BOUQUETS & BUCKLES

Elliott Rose

kensingtonbooks.com

KENSINGTON BOOKS are published by:

Kensington Publishing Corp.
900 Third Avenue
New York, NY 10022

kensingtonbooks.com

Copyright © 2024 by Elliott Rose

This book is a work of fiction. Names, characters, businesses, organizations, places, events, and incidents either are the product of the author's imagination or are used fictitiously. Any resemblance to actual persons, living or dead, events, or locales is entirely coincidental.

To the extent that the image or images on the cover of this book depict a person or persons, such person or persons are merely models, and are not intended to portray any character or characters featured in the book.

All rights reserved. No part of this book may be reproduced in any form or by any means without the prior written consent of the Publisher, excepting brief quotes used in reviews.

Without limiting the author's and publisher's exclusive rights, any unauthorized use of this publication to train generative artificial intelligence (AI) technologies is expressly prohibited.

All Kensington titles, imprints, and distributed lines are available at special quantity discounts for bulk purchases for sales promotions, premiums, fundraising, educational, or institutional use.

Special book excerpts or customized printings can also be created to fit specific needs. For details, write or phone the office of the Kensington sales manager: Kensington Publishing Corp., 900 Third Avenue, New York, NY 10022, attn: Sales Department; phone 1-800-221-2647.

The K with book logo Reg US Pat. & TM Off.

First Kensington Trade Paperback Printing: August 2025

ISBN 978-1-4967-5891-0 (trade paperback)

10 9 8 7 6 5 4 3 2 1

Printed in United States of America

Electronic edition: ISBN 978-1-4967-5896-5

Interior art by Cosmic Imprint Publishing
Author photograph by Elliott Rose

The authorized representative in the EU for product safety and compliance
is eucomply OU, Parnu mnt 139b-14, Apt 123
Tallinn, Berlin 11317, hello@eucompliancepartner.com

For those who don't want a lot for Christmas...
other than a hot cowboy, and multiple orgasms.

Hello dear reader,

Welcome to Christmas Eve in Crimson Ridge...

This novella is a best friend's dad, snowed in, cowboy romance with a happily ever after.

Content Notes

PLEASE SCAN THE CODE BELOW:

My website has a full list of Content notes,
including a chapter by chapter break down if required.
ELLIOTTROSEAUTHOR.COM

Please note, you can email ELLIOTTROSE.PA@GMAIL.COM
for more information or clarification.

The Playlist

Good Luck, Babe . Chappell Roan

Guy For That . Post Malone, Luke Combs

On A Different Night . Josh Ross

Whiskey On You . Nate Smith

Don't Mind If I Do . Riley Green, Ella Langley

Underneath the tree . Kelly Clarkson

Tennessee Whiskey . teddy swimss

Christmas In The Country . Thomas Rhett

Falll In Love . Bailey Zimmerman

Highway . Shaboozey

You Make It Feel Like Christmas . Gwen Stefani, Blake Shelton

Chapter 1

Skylar

It's the most wonderful time of the year.

Yeah... when you don't work in retail, events, or hospitality, it's fucking peachy. However, when you've been run off your feet for the past few weeks making sure that everyone else has a magical, glittering Christmas, your own plans for nothing more than curling up in front of the fire and spending most of the time naked with nowhere to go and no one to talk to sounds mighty appealing.

So that's why I currently have my go-to nineties grunge playlist on blast, and my very special *hot as fuck* outfit on, after high-tailing it out of town at the first opportunity to escape.

I locked the door to my cute-as-a-button florist shop the second my final customers for the year headed out that door.

Bless their sweet little mulled wine offerings, nope very much, and desire to chit-chat about what plans I have, eating and sleeping, but I practically stuffed their last-minute Christmas Eve order into their hands—lord help me not to have to see a single sprig of holly or mistletoe, let alone another festive wreath for the next eleven months—and damn near sprinted to my car.

Checking my hair in the rearview, I cruise along the empty main boulevard of Crimson Ridge. The place is all twinkling lights and small-town charm, with a giant outdoor Christmas tree erected in the square. Festive cheer of grandiose proportions proudly greets me as I make my return for the first time in twelve months.

My hometown.

The sweetest little middle-of-nowhere-Montana winter destination, where nothing much happens, and the population is pretty much exclusively ranchers and cowboys.

Which is why I made the decision to move to the next town over after college, where my teeny tiny little florist business actually had a hope in hell of surviving her first year of being open.

As much as I would love to still live here, with the gorgeous Victorian-style buildings, trees lining the middle of the wide main street, and everyone-knows-everyone kind of vibe... there isn't much foot traffic. Certainly not enough to sustain luxuries like bouquets and floral arrangements in a place like this.

I'd be better off selling horse feed and leather polish if I was in it solely for the money.

It feels strangely familiar, driving past all the shops and locations ingrained in me from my younger years. Places that haven't changed, yet the years have rolled on by.

Even stranger is the realization that I don't have a reason to come back here anymore, now that my parents have left town, selling up everything to buy an RV and begin living the gray nomad life.

Love that for them; it's utterly stinking adorable.

They're currently sending me daily photos and awkward but cute selfies from the other end of the country, chasing the sunshine and warmth of a non-winter in California while the rest of us here are buried up to our necks in snow.

Which is pretty much the standard backdrop for Crimson Ridge at this time of year. I wasn't even sure I'd be able to make it over here on Christmas Eve, but the weather gods have played nice and given me the perfect window of opportunity to surprise Jeremy. He's here house-sitting for his parents, and the drive to the Smith family home is as familiar as the back of my hand.

The cul-de-sac his folks' house is located on stands lined with plenty of trees, and I use that to disguise my arrival… I mean, my boyfriend thinks I'm currently picking up Christmas Eve takeout before heading back to my apartment, where I told him I'd be getting ready to facemask and video chat once I've curled up on my couch with a glass of wine in hand.

Not that I'm actually here in town, about to surprise him.

Pulling off to the side of the road a couple of houses up the block, allows me to park my car where it can't be seen. Out here in this neighborhood, it's all cute festive decor, with lawn ornaments and garland lights festooned over the houses, making the dark Christmas Eve night a whole lot brighter.

I grin to myself, pulling out my favorite magenta lipstick and twist the rearview mirror in order to paint my lips. The shade goes perfectly with the waves framing my face of my pastel pink bob. The thought of turning up to surprise Jere when we didn't think either of us would be able to see the other for the holiday season—with how busy I had been at the shop, not to mention the snow often being too heavy to get to Crimson Ridge—sends a curl of excitement through my stomach.

This will be our first proper Christmas as a couple, after dating for the past three months, and to be able to burst through that door and hug him has been the only fucking thing getting me through all the insanely long hours I've worked this past week.

Grabbing my coat, I bundle myself up and figure I'll do the *surprise* part with his gift first. I can come back, get my bag, and move my car into the driveway later.

As I slide out of the door, the air has that weird energy to it. Too calm, too still. Experience tells me tonight is on the verge of starting to snow prolifically and turn everything into a real-life snow globe. So I cradle the jar of his favorite peanut butter cookies against my chest, duck my chin into my collar, and scuttle my ass and cute boots down the sidewalk.

Jere's house has the curtains shut out front, but I can see lights on. As I slip around the side towards the back door, there's music playing, the closer I get the more the anticipation builds.

I've always been the 'single one' over the holidays, and this year, it settles something inside me to know that for the first time, I won't be alone.

The back door has a glass panel built in, and looks into the open-plan kitchen area, all aglow with lights switched on over the kitchen island. I roll my lips together with eager excitement when I see Jere standing on the far side of the room.

He's looking down, his gaze fixed on something I can't see. Light brown hair flops over his forehead, those metal rim glasses giving him that scholarly hottie vibe, but there is an unusualness in his expression. Enough so, that it makes me pause before I reach out to grab the door handle.

I see the way his hand moves, partially obscured by the countertop.

Something about this scene isn't right. The fine hairs on the back of my neck stand on end, not because of the winter's air, but because if I didn't know any better, he's mouthing words.

If I didn't know any better...

Oh god.

That's when the entire damn script flips right before my disbelieving eyes.

The reason his hand is doing something becomes apparent. Dumping realization on me, cold and brutally sudden, like a slab of snow falling off the roof.

It's fisted in some bitch's hair.

Her glossy blonde head comes into view as he drags her to stand up.

She's been down there on her knees.

Jesus. This fucking asshole has got some other girl blowing him in the kitchen.

On Christmas Eve, no less.

My chest goes numb, and I stumble backward, still not wanting to believe the cock-sucking evidence right in front of me.

And that's when he shoves his tongue in her mouth.

CHAPTER 2

My toes and the balls of my feet don't have any sensation left in them. Neither do my fingers. Neither does the cavity left hollowed out inside my chest.

Fumbling in my jacket pocket for my keys, I'm like a shadow in the night, disappearing back toward my car as fast as I can fucking move.

Humiliation has kicked my heart out into the snow, leaving it to freeze amongst the rows of illuminated reindeer and gaudy candy canes.

The backs of my eyes sting, and I'm about two seconds from bursting into a torrent of ugly, snotty tears.

What a piece of shit.

Is there a worse way to spend your Christmas than discovering by accident that your boyfriend has been fucking around behind your back?

As I dash across the curb to reach the driver's door and get myself the hell out of here, I nearly collapse at the sight before me.

Oh my fucking god. Not right now. No, please, no.

The front tire on my car is as deflated as my stomped-on little heart. Sitting flaccid and drooped, helpfully lit up for me to see that I cannot possibly drive away from here by the array of red flashing Christmas lights on the fence of the house I parked in front of.

That's the moment the waterworks erupt.

Fuck this. Fuck it all. Fuck Jere and whatever slut he's been secretly banging down here in Crimson Ridge every time he needed to come and 'house sit,' ... which, now that I think about it, was a lot.

Ugh. I'm so tired and can't even process what the hell I've done to deserve a night like this.

With fat tears rolling down my cheeks, I slide into the driver's seat and grab my cell. Stabbing at my contacts list, I know Brad will save my ass. He'll come rescue me, cuddle me, and let me watch a rom-com marathon while bundled under a blanket on his sofa. If there is any man I can count on to have enough booze and ice cream to drown my every last sorrow through the duration of the holidays, it's him.

Bradford Rhodes will also know how to change a tire because he was raised on a ranch, and as much as I'd love to claim to be *Miss Independent*, I simply do not.

My knee bounces. The phone rings several times. Just when I think he's not going to pick up, to my relief, the line connects.

I don't even wait, launching straight into full melt-down mode, blurting out everything through sniffles and hiccups.

"Brad... he's such a douchebag... cheated on me... you were right all along... I can't believe I was so fucking blind... and now, I'm stuck on the side of the road with a flat tire, and it's about to snow like crazy leaving me stuck here on Christmas Eve, and god help me, I will die if he realizes I'm out here... please, please say you can rescue me from this living hell?" I sniff loudly, wiping tears away with the heel of my palm.

"Skylar?" The gritty-sounding voice in my ear makes me do a double take.

"Brad?"

"Skylar, is everything ok?" The voice on the other end of the line is most definitely *not* Brad. It doesn't sound like Flinn, his boyfriend, either.

My eyes are blurry with tears when I pull the phone away, and my hand flies to my mouth when I see the name lit up on screen.

Brad's Dad.

Oh shit. Oh shit.

I just accidentally sobbing-dialed my life long, cannot ever stop swooning over, hottest man in existence, cowboy crush.

My best friend's father.

"Skylar, what's going on?" His voice echoes through the quiet of my car.

"I'm so sorry, Mr. Rhodes. I didn't mean to disturb you. I meant to call Brad."

"You're upset." He ignores my feeble words.

"Uhhh, it's nothing. Don't worry. I'm hanging up now. Hope you have a lovely Christmas." My heart is in my throat. I want to bury myself in a shallow grave alongside Rudolph.

"Don't even think about it. Where are you?" His voice sounds a little rough, like he'd maybe been sleeping, and that makes me wince harder. My damp cheeks grow hot with the embarrassment of everything colliding together in the worst possible sequence of events.

"I'm over on Jones Avenue, but honestly, please erase this from your memory, forget this call even happened. I'm so sorry my thumb must have slipped and hit your contact."

Fuck my life. My eyes squeeze shut, and I lean my head forward against the steering wheel. I can already taste the sweet burn of whiskey and salted caramel ice cream that I know

Brad cannot survive without. That boy always has a gallon of the good stuff stashed in his freezer.

"Are you inside your car?"

"Yes. Honestly, I'll be fine, I—"

The line scuffles a little and he cuts me off. "Turn your ignition on and keep the heating running, otherwise you'll freeze. Give me ten minutes."

That makes my eyes pop open. What?

"Oh, no... no, you really don't have to—"

The man doesn't allow me to finish speaking.

"Skylar, I'm already in my truck and on my way. Stay put."

With that, he hangs up on me.

CHAPTER 3

Lucas

What the hell am I doing?

It's nine at night on Christmas Eve, and I'm driving through empty streets to offer a helping hand to my son's best friend—to assist with whatever emergency situation she's gotten herself into.

A girl who I haven't seen in a year.

Not since she was back in Crimson Ridge last holiday season, and certainly the last person on this planet who I expected would be calling me.

Adding to all that, she's in tears.

I didn't catch most of what she rattled off over the phone—must have dropped off to sleep on the couch after I finished up with the horses for the night—and I was only half awake when I answered her call.

Doesn't matter. I don't need the hows or whys; the girl is clearly in some kind of distress, and sitting on the side of the road when snow's about to roll through at any moment and cut off the town... well, she couldn't have picked a worse time to have a flat.

Worst timing? Or best timing?

Holy fuck. No. I scrub one hand over my mouth. Don't even fucking think like that for one second. She's Brad's best friend, his same age, and spent half her teenage years round the ranch while the two of them grew up together.

That puts her in the *don't even goddamn think about it, you old perv* category.

The only problem is that Skylar is very much now a *woman*, and Jesus, if I didn't see that far too easily this time last year. It was impossible not to notice how much she'd matured and grown into herself. How animated she was talking about her new business. Brad had invited her, after taking it upon himself to organize a New Year's Eve party. Which, to no one's surprise, he's doing again these holidays.

Supposedly, he tells me with that smile of his that asks for forgiveness rather than permission, it's great promotion for the ranch.

What do I know? I'm good for training horses and that's about the only thing I've ever known.

Brad's the one who understands crap like networking and marketing and *branding*. All the parts of modern-day ranching I'm terrible at, whereas my son and his boyfriend are goddamn naturals at those kinds of things, and I'm fucking grateful they're here to handle that side of the business.

Then again, my kid is a social fucking butterfly, so he lives for that kind of shit. He certainly didn't inherit those genes from me.

Thinking back to almost a year ago, I wish I could blame liquor for the fact I noticed her when I shouldn't have, but I'd offered to be a sober driver for folks coming along that night. There wasn't a drop of drink in me, so I couldn't put it down to anything other than being out of my damn mind. As if being twice her age wasn't reason enough to stop seeking her out wherever she floated around the room, the stone-cold reality is I should know better than to be staring at my son's best friend.

Skylar caught my eye and threw my whole world off center and then to top it all off I even drove her home just after midnight.

We barely exchanged two words, and all I remember is white-knuckling the steering wheel the entire way in an effort to prevent me from making a goddamn fool of myself.

When we pulled up outside her parent's old house on Oakwood, however, I could have sworn she hovered in the truck, painted fingernails resting on the handle.

Coulda sworn she opened her mouth as if to say something, but then thought better of it and bolted out the door into the darkness, and back out of my life.

At the time, I rationalized that it was absolutely, one hundred percent, for the best that I was most likely not going to see her again for a very long time, outside of her and Brad getting together for something or other that might make our paths cross momentarily.

Now here I am, twelve months later, and the young woman, who a man like me has no business thinking about, is the reason I'm driving across town.

It dawns on me as I pull into the cul-de-sac where she's stranded that her folks don't live in town anymore. Last I heard, they sold up everything and went traveling.

Fuck.

Annnnd, I'm guessing she doesn't know, or has forgotten maybe, that Brad isn't here either. He's gone to spend Christmas with Flinn's family.

Double fuck.

As I pull into the street, I see her car straight away. The same little silver hatchback she's had since she turned eighteen and headed off to college with my son.

Now I've gotta figure out what I'm going to do with a girl who won't be able to go anywhere until I help her change that tire this late at night on Christmas Eve. Not to mention that the snow has already started piling up in the time it has taken me to drive over here.

Or, more to the point, I've got to figure out how to stop my dick from being ready to leap to attention at the mere thought of this girl nearly twenty years younger than me.

CHAPTER 4

Skylar

Headlights sweep over my vehicle from behind, lighting up the fluffy, white evidence of snowfall that has started coming down thick and fast in the time I've sat here waiting for Lucas Rhodes to arrive.

Nearly crawling out of my skin the entire time.

About ten times, I've seen something out of the corner of my eye and nearly had a heart attack, thinking that it was Jeremy or his side bitch ready to appear at my window and catch me in the act of lurking down the street.

My pulse thuds a frantic, unsteady beat in my neck. In the rearview, I see a big truck pull up, and the headlights cut off. The driver's door swings open, boots hit the gathered snow, revealing my every cowboy fantasy and teenage girl obsession who strides through the elements toward me.

Jeans fitted to perfection. High collar weatherproof jacket. Of course, he's got his requisite *Lucas Rhodes* felt cowboy hat on his head.

The man is cut straight from a romance novel, and yet somehow has remained single in all the years I've known his son.

He even has his own ranch, runs horses, and does *cowboy things* as and when the other larger properties around here need help.

I quickly brush my hands over my hair to smooth down any strays. Have I got eyeliner running all down my face? God. This is humiliating.

My best friend's dad has had to come rescue me on Christmas Eve. Would the ground kindly do a gal a solid and swallow me up? Better yet, can I just fast-forward out of this nightmare and wake up in my own bed so this can all be over?

As he draws level with the passenger side, I do a painfully awkward wave and grimace.

He gestures for me to roll the window down, then leans a forearm on the door as he bends to look in on my misery.

"Stay there. Don't want you catching a cold." He cuts straight to the point. No smiles, giving me only a display of cheekbones and a short beard to make a girl weep. "Pop your trunk; I'll get the spare."

Shiiiiit.

"Um. You're standing right beside it." If I hadn't already cried my eyes out before, I would be tempted now. How could I forget? I had been meaning to replace it since getting a flat just as winter started, only to wind up endlessly run off my feet with the shop. I never got around to it, and now I want to smack myself in the jaw for sounding like the dumbest bitch alive.

"You ain't carrying a spare?"

I wilt as fast as a dehydrated petal under his dark gaze. His eyes like night study me from beneath the brim of his hat, no doubt chewing silently on my stupidity.

"No. I'm so sorry, Mr. Rhodes. I tried calling Brad after you, and he's not answering, and I'm..." This is the moment. The moment I run out of words. What am I actually going to do? This town shuts up shop for the holidays, nothing is open, and

I'll bet all of the options for accommodation are displaying *No Vacancy* signs, thanks to the festive season.

He pokes his tongue against the inside of his cheek for a moment. No doubt thinking I'm the human equivalent of a dumpster fire. Meanwhile I'm sitting in the front seat, wearing an outfit that is definitely not appropriate for spending time with a man old enough to be my father.

Hell, he's friendly with my parents. A little younger than them, but they know each other all the same.

"This your stuff?" He jerks his chin toward the weekender sitting on the backseat.

I nod. Feeling numb and helpless.

"Lock up. Get in the truck."

Without elaborating, he opens the door, grabs hold of my bag, and then steps back, waiting for me to rediscover how to use my brain. He stands there filling the sidewalk with snow dusting his broad shoulders, white flecks settle against the dark rim of his hat, and doesn't move.

Meanwhile, I'm stuck in place, not processing what is happening here.

So when the rugged cowboy of my silly little dreams stoops to peer at me through the open window for a second time, my heart zooms around inside my chest at his next words.

"You're coming home with me."

CHAPTER 5

Lucas

What am I supposed to do in a situation like this? If I attempted to offload my son's best friend to some random motel in Crimson Ridge—right on Christmas—what kind of person would that make me? That's the kind of shit reserved for heartless fucking bastards.

Skylar doesn't have anywhere to go, and I'm sure as hell not going to abandon her all alone.

However, is the prospect of bringing her back to my house, my ranch, with the way the snow is sticking on the ground, going to be the greatest test of my sanity... most likely, yes.

I've yet to grill her about what I'm sure I heard her say over the phone just before. Even though I might have been still foggy with sleep, I know what she said down the line between her tears.

He's such a douchebag... cheated on me.

Exactly like the last time we sat in this truck together, the drive has been silent. She doesn't seem keen to talk, and I'm shit with words on a good day. Too many years on my own and too much time with only horses for company, as Brad likes to remind me.

Except, everything changes the moment we pull into the long drive winding toward the house. Out of the corner of my eye, I see her sit up a little straighter and take in the snow-covered trees and the sloping track leading to the stables. In front of us stands my simple property, nothing fancy but it's home all the same, with a wooden porch wrapped around the outside. Steps run along one side that I can remember her and a group of their friends from high school spending hours sitting on playing music and being kids together during the summers.

"I'd forgotten how this place always looks so pretty." She breathes, taking in the swirling snowflakes reflected in the headlights, and the glow of the house from where I'd left the lights on.

Yeah, I'll agree with her on that. The only problem is that I'm certainly not looking at any of the sights outside this truck.

I don't run a big property, enough for my own horses and ones that belong to others that I stable here on their behalf. During the warmer months of the year, I'll offer training clinics and riding lessons, and some of the local rodeo guys and girls come use the place for their offseason practices. Brad and Flinn have their own cabin over by the barn and yards situated beyond the house, over the back.

While having my son here working the ranch is great and all, he's an adult, and I'm happiest in my own company. Our living arrangement gives all of us enough distance that we're not on top of each other.

That boy sure as hell loves to tease me that I wouldn't survive without him, which is bullshit, but it's easier having the two of them live on the ranch; I'll grant him that. Even if they do love to steal my beer and help themselves to my fridge while they're at it.

I pull up out front of the porch and cut the engine as Skylar keeps looking around with wide eyes like I've driven us into some sort of fairytale or some shit.

"Winter looks gorgeous out here."

God, I can't fucking get my head on straight. She sounds so relieved, so happy to be here, and that's screwing with my already very messed up thoughts.

Something bucks around inside my chest and tries to crow about how good she looks here, too. With that pastel pink hair skimming her jaw, shorter than when she was in that passenger seat a year ago, but it suits her even more at this length. It highlights that pixie, heart-shaped face, perfectly framing those baby blue eyes of hers.

"Let's get inside, get you warm. This snow is gonna keep piling up." Coughing into my fist, I keep my eyes firmly on the house, the porch, anywhere but the gorgeous girl filling the cab of my truck with her feminine scent.

"Thank you so much again, Mr. Rhodes."

Jesus. I both love and loathe the fact she's calling me that. It collides inside my head with the force of two bulls charging one another. The fucked up part of my brain enjoys it more than I want to dare examine. The other part of me wants her to call me by my first name, because, at this stage, I'd do damn near anything to erase any lingering evidence of boundaries.

"Don't mention it." My jaw is almost frozen in place.

Do I dare admit the truth to myself? That I'd be tempted to discard my morals real quick if it meant being able to eliminate those infuriating invisible lines stretching between us. You know, ones that relate to our difference in ages, or the plain and simple fact she's my kid's best friend.

Staying in my seat is a bad idea.

I make the move to hop out and grab her bag from the back, but she beats me to it and our gazes lock from where we're standing in the open doors facing one another from opposite sides of the vehicle.

From here I get my first proper look at Skylar. I get to really look at her, and there might as well be a bronc's hoofprint on my chest judging by the way air struggles to reach my lungs.

Her cheeks are a little flushed, plump lips painted a stunning shade of pink that, on someone else, might look ridiculous, but on Skylar, it's perfectly balanced with the sweetness of her pastel hair and hot as fuck silver ring in the center of her nose. A *septum piercing*, as I was informed by Brad, mid eye-roll, when I fumbled around completely tongue tied seeing her with it for the first time last year.

He thought I didn't know what kids these days call that kind of thing, when really all I knew was that she caught me off-guard turning up at the house looking like a dream I hadn't dared to believe existed.

Now, here she is. Catching me unprepared to navigate the way my attraction to her hasn't faded in the slightest.

Clusters of puffy white settle on top of her wavy curls as delicate snowflakes, making her look like some sort of winter fairy that I've been gifted as a Christmas miracle.

Goddamn, why does this girl have to be so insanely attractive?

It might be snowing, the air swirling thick around us, but neither of us seems to be able to move, and that's when her eyes waver. They dip behind those thick lashes, and if I wasn't already aware of the thundering rhythm caged inside my ribs, that beat becomes erratic as all hell.

Her blue eyes drop to my mouth.

My fist grips the door to the truck so hard I'm sure the frame is going to buckle.

I'm not imagining this.

I'm not hallucinating.

Skylar's tongue pokes out to wet her lips, and we both stand there like statues. Neither wanting to make the first move to break whatever unspoken connection this is.

Only, the outside world decides to choose that moment to invade our privacy.

Her cell phone bursts to life in her coat pocket.

CHAPTER 6
Skylar

"**O**h my god, Sky... are you ok? I've got like fifty missed calls and you didn't leave a single message. Way to freak me out." Brad's voice booms down the phone when I answer.

Across from me, the cowboy who I'd just been locked in the most intense moment of... *I don't even know what that was...* slams his door and strides toward the front porch.

Whitewashed boards, worn down in places where countless boots have stepped on them over time, a particular spot that holds a thousand memories from when I would hang out here as a teenager.

A teenager with a big, fat, secret crush.

"Hey B, I'm ok now." With one shoulder, I clamp my phone against my ear, carrying my bags as I follow his bootprints left in the soft powder coating the gravel.

"Do I need to send out a search party, or call a lawyer, or post bail, or what?"

"Nah, you can stand down. Crisis averted for the moment." My eyes drift up to the open doorway and the broad shoulders waiting just inside. The man holding the door for me because that's the kind of thing this man does without question. The cowboy who ended up being my knight in shining armor, after all.

"Did you make it to Crimson Ridge, ok? The weather turned to shit over here real quick tonight."

"Over here? Where are you?" Walking into the Rhodes home feels as natural as anything. I know every nook and cranny in this house, and there's something comforting in the fact it hasn't changed hardly at all that I can see at first glance.

"We're spending Christmas with Flinn's family this year, remember?"

Oh, shit.

"Sorry, crown me world's crappiest friend right now. Totally forgot you guys were heading out of town for the holidays."

"I'll forgive you. Can't blame you for forgetting, considering the fact you didn't sleep and made like five thousand Christmas wreaths in two weeks, Sky. Crazy bitch workaholic that you most certainly are." He chuckles in that deep voice that reminds me of weekends spent teasing each other and driving back roads with the windows rolled down, blasting Nirvana, and daydreaming of bright futures for what our lives might bring.

I'm standing in the entrance hall, knowing exactly how many steps it takes to reach the guest room at the top of the staircase to my left. A room that I've stayed in too many times to count over the years. Yet, I don't make a move. Something about *this* particular visit, when Brad isn't here, changes things.

"So why were you blowing up my phone, bestie? Do I need to egg a certain wank face's house when I get back?"

Scrunching my eyes, I brace myself for the inevitable. "Yeah... so... you were right about him. The guy was cheating on me." I say that last part as hushed as possible, because I don't know where Brad's father has disappeared off to inside the house after shutting the door behind me, and I also feel insanely embarrassed at the prospect of having to discuss the truth behind my road-side-rescue.

"Bitch, I knew it." The phone rustles as Brad does something on the other end of the line. "Flinn, babe, I told you," he hollers in the background.

"Ok, ok, you don't have to alert the entire village." I hiss.

There's a pause while he mutters something under his breath and hums in agreement. "Flinn says he wants you to know that *'he knew it'* too, by the way."

"Well, aren't you both just a pair of clair-fucking-voyants."

"Our powers extend beyond bi-panic and having excellent style, you know." He clicks his tongue at me. "Wait... so, if you're in Crimson Ridge... but you've ditched Jere-prick-face..."

Shit. Here it comes.

"Um, so I might be standing in your house."

"Huh?"

Words tumble out as I give Brad the rundown of my shitty night while shifting in place awkwardly in the entrance. It's set back a little from the open-plan farmhouse kitchen, and as I fidget on the spot, I still don't know where the man of the house has vanished to.

"God, Sky, I'm so sorry..." he groans. "But, I'm warning you now, Dad's probably gonna insist on his incredibly lame, old man Christmas routine. Where he plonks his ass in a chair reading by the fire and alternates that with going to sleep, snoring, and just being super boring in general."

A smirk threatens to escape onto my lips because Brad should know by now that is one hundred percent the perfect sounding day for me. My best friend is the social butterfly extrovert out of the two of us, and right now, curling up in front of the fire with a book sounds like my kinda heaven, Christmas or otherwise.

That quite possibly might be the perfect solution as I wait

for the snow to clear, in order to soothe my bruised ego, thanks to Jeremy and his kitchen blow job, and recharge my drained social battery after the craziness of the shop.

"I fucking heard that." A gruff voice appears in front of me.

"Actually, maybe it's kinda perfect, you two can both hate Christmas together." Brad lets out a hearty laugh down the line. "Take good care of my girl, won't ya, Dad?" He says loud enough for him to hear.

I'm internally dying at this entire situation.

Why yes, I would very much like to be taken care of by this slab of cowboy.

"Merry Christmas, guys." It's impossible to miss the way those dark eyes lock on mine as he replies to Brad.

"Yeah, you too. I'll give you a call tomorrow, and we'll aim to be back once the snow has cleared in a couple of days."

We say our goodbyes, and by the time I hang the phone up, I'm squirming beneath the weight of this man's stare.

He's stripped out of his outdoor gear to reveal a faded denim shirt pushed to his elbows. Those jeans he wears the hell out of are far too easy to appreciate up close.

Lucas Rhodes has reached his forties, but is the epitome of a man who could easily pass for much younger than that. It's only the dusting of gray at his temples, the salt and pepper beard, matched with a sexy white streak that has always curled through the front of his disheveled hair that belies his age.

I've swooned over that rogue lock of white in amongst the longer dark strands falling across his forehead for more years than I can remember.

"Let me take your coat." His voice comes out husky and I swear to god my knees buckle a little.

He steps around to stand behind me, and our height difference is marked at this proximity. I barely reach the man's chest, even in my heeled boots.

I'm a curvy girl with thick thighs, a soft stomach, and tits I wish were bigger to give me more of an hourglass shape. I know how to dress in order to feel myself, yet, no matter what, there's no disguising the fact I'm short.

Standing with this man at my back, I feel dwarfed by his size. He's thick-chested. Broad and muscled. The kind of steadiness to him, that is a constant reminder of how strong and sturdy he is, with absolutely no interest in being cut or showing off.

This is a man who has a body capable of hard graft and days on end working with his horses and the land.

God, I've got to get my ovaries under control and stop drooling over this cowboy.

Only, he keeps making it nearly impossible to do so. Strong fingers hook beneath my coat collar as I undo the buttons. And that's when I remember.

The outfit I've got on underneath.

CHAPTER 7

H oly shit.
    The soft wool of Skylar's black coat gives way, allowing me to peel it off her shoulders.

I mean, this girl has a figure to fucking crawl across hot coals for, and I don't know how the fuck we've ended up here, but I say a silent curse.

She's fucking stunning, and what she's wearing... well, if I wasn't already battling an erection, I damn well am now.

My gaze should *not* be roaming everywhere at once like I've never laid eyes on a woman before, but I can't fucking help it. Her black leather skirt barely covers her lush ass, with sheer black tights skimming down those thighs I want to squeeze until she whimpers for me. Her top is also black, but you wouldn't know it because the damn thing is entirely see-through, and from here, I can already see the thin strap and clasp reaching across her spine that tells me she's only wearing a bra underneath.

I'm not sure I'm gonna survive the moment this girl turns around, and I see how her tits are showcased beneath that tempting layer of sheer fabric.

Beneath the long sleeve of her cropped top—if you could even call it a top—are the colorful designs I've only ever dared to sneak small glimpses of in the times I've been in the same room as her. The adult version of my son's best friend.

After Skylar went off to art college with Brad, she started sporting more and more ink each time she returned to Crimson Ridge during the holidays.

Like everything with this girl, it's hot, she's hot, and now that I can glimpse them up close there's a mix of florals and colors and patterns tracking from the curve of her shoulders down to her wrists. I want to ask her about what kind of meaning they hold for the dichotomy of a girl. Who wears her hair the color of sweet fairy floss and favors chunky black boots.

Skylar has grown into a woman who is a whole lot of gorgeous, and a mystery at the same time.

"Help yourself to a drink, you know where everything is." I practically choke out the words. *Do not keep staring at her ass.* "I'll hang your coat up and drop your bags upstairs... same room as always, yeah?"

She turns her chin to peek back at me over one shoulder, all heavy lashes and pretty pink lips.

"Thanks, Mr. Rhodes."

My cock fucking leaps to life. "Just Luke is fine. Probably should have pulled you up on that years ago."

"Ok." There's that same breathiness in her voice again. "Can I get you a drink, too?"

Yup. Just hand me the entire goddamn bottle at this point.

"Sure. Whiskey's good for me." I say, taking the opportunity to busy myself with mundane things like hanging her coat and depositing her bag upstairs and trying my best to avoid thinking about the fact I'm going to be stuck in this house with Skylar, alone.

CHAPTER 8

My tits and ass are literally hanging out, and I'm pouring my best friend's dad a whiskey.

Meanwhile, I've already knocked back a generous pour, the burn sliding a long trail straight down to my belly.

I don't know what the fuck to think, or feel. Right now, I'm entirely messed up because I could have sworn Lucas Rhodes—Luke—stared at me while I was on the phone to his son with something dangerously similar to desire in his eyes.

Then he offered to take my coat for me, and there was no denying the heat twisting and turning between us when he hovered at my back.

Am I reading into every little detail? Maybe.

Am I feeling reckless enough to see what this outfit might strike a match and set fire to? Absolutely.

Why not allow myself the chance to reach out and sample a taste of the forbidden? It is Christmas, after all. We're snowed in together here. As soon as I can get a new tire fitted, as soon as the roads clear, I'm going back home and really have no reason to come back to Crimson Ridge again for the foreseeable future.

Brad doesn't need to know.

I'm in the mood to be a whole lot irresponsible, and the cowboy I'm stuck in this house with is the kind of temptation a girl like me has thought about too many times over the years.

He's never once been inappropriate or ever acted in a way with me that might have blurred lines. Always being the perfect gentleman, driving any of us home late at night if we ever needed a ride. Always making sure we had his cell number in case of an emergency.

Lucas Rhodes is one heck of a good man, an excellent father, and has always supported Brad.

The cowboy I've swooned over in secret for *years* has always been the kind of distant daydream. The fantasy riding in on horseback, I've only ever laid in bed at night and drifted off thinking wicked thoughts about. The forbidden temptation dressed in jeans that should be illegal and with a charcoal color hat that makes my knees go weak.

And hell, if it doesn't make it even hotter that now we're both here in a moment when life has turned on its head, and I'm here in this house as a fully consenting adult who most definitely would like to loosen his buckle and worship this man's dick, if he'll let me.

Bracing myself against the wooden top of the central island, I look down at my tits. The girls are fully on display, rounded, and threatening to spill over the top of the black harness bra I treated myself to as an early Christmas lingerie purchase. My sheer cropped top is nothing but a flashing neon sign directing attention towards my cleavage.

Little did I know the first man who would see the magical powers of silky fabric and lace would be nearly twice my age. A rugged cowboy who shouldn't know how fabulous my tits look in this outfit, but holy fuck, do I want him to.

I've never been this person.

I've never dared to act like this before.

So maybe the snow and the chaos of emotions running rampant through my veins, along with that shot of whiskey, maybe that's what gives me the courage to do the thing I would never normally think of doing in a million years.

As I hear heavy footsteps coming down the steps, I grab the bottle and two glasses, scooting around to the side of the extremely manly, chunky dining table facing the entranceway. Pushing one of the chairs slightly aside, I hoist myself up and plonk my ass on the wooden slab.

My stomach fills with butterflies as his heavy footfall reaches the last stair.

Something has been hanging in the air tonight, like the snowflakes drifting outside the kitchen windows. Something a teeny bit magical, that sizzles with potential, and if I didn't know any better, might just be the once-in-a-lifetime opportunity I'll be able to dream about for years to come.

If there's one thing I'm going to do to get over the turmoil of tonight, it's shoot my shot.

CHAPTER 9

I didn't really know what to expect walking back into the kitchen. Maybe to be offering Skylar some dinner, or to have a discussion about whatever had upset her earlier, or to make fucking small talk about the fact we're going to be stuck here together on my ranch until the snow melts.

You know, to be filling the role of *Brad's father* that I've been for as long as I've known her.

What I didn't expect was to find her perched on my dining table, looking like a goddamn wet dream.

Well, fuck.

The sight I'd been steeling myself for while pacing upstairs comes into sharp focus as I walk into the soft glow thrown across the room by the overhead lights. My kitchen has turned into an illicit stage show, where there used to be innocent hanging pendant lighting, it's now become a warm spotlight caressing her every curve—highlighting the fact I can see straight through her shirt.

It stops me in my tracks, and I have to scrub a hand over my face. There's no way to disguise my reaction, this girl is so fucking gorgeous, and there's only one reason she's perched herself like that.

Her skirt is short, hugging her thighs, barely covering her from the waist down, and it takes everything to not look at the spot where the material ends and her tights disappear beneath the hem.

But looking up in the direction of her face is no better because this girl's tits are enough to break me. The way they're wrapped up and perfectly presented... she was obviously dressing for *someone* tonight, and I'm guessing it's whichever jerk off left her crying and stranded on the side of the road.

"Skylar, what are you doing?" My voice is scratchy. I know exactly what she's doing, but my brain cannot process what my eyes are seeing. A part of me says that I should tell her to get down from there and should show her where the leftovers are so she can reheat something.

On one hand, the sensible, boring, fatherly part of me attempts to be *good*.

Then, there's the other guy.

He's the asshole who is beyond tempted to see whether this girl might enjoy a bit of fun. Who is desperate for a taste of the young woman he's been stuck with *un-fatherly* thoughts about for the past year.

"You wanted a drink, didn't you?" She bites down on her lower lip and offers me a glass.

Like a magnet, I'm drawn forward. Slowly crossing the last remaining space separating us and stopping just in front of her knees.

"A drink, yes. But *this*..." I nod at the seductive little perch she's seated on. "This isn't just a drink, is it?" As I take the glass from her, our knuckles brush, and that innocent point of contact feels fucking electrified.

"Do you want it to be just a drink, Luke?" She flutters heavy eyelashes my way and leans back on her palms.

Goddamn, I want to hear how my name sounds on her lips when she's moaning for me and begging to come.

"That's all it *should* be, and you know it." My throat bobs a heavy swallow.

"What if we didn't know each other? Let's say I'd never been here. We'd never met before. We're just two adults who happen to be snowed in together. Would there be any *shoulds* or *should nots* between us then?"

Christ, if the conditions outside weren't a total whiteout, I should be excusing myself to go down to the barn, cool the fuck off, and busy my hands with the horses or shit like that. Instead, I'm locked in this illicit bubble and can't find it within myself to step away.

"I don't know. It's hard to say when you've obviously had other plans for Christmas based on that outfit you've got on."

Pausing to take a sip of whiskey, I let my eyes hold her baby blues.

Something wavers in her energy. "It's ok. I can go change. We can hang out if that's all you want." The way she says those words, it's like she's already preparing herself for rejection, and I hate that this girl immediately assumes she wouldn't be wanted when it's only my own hang ups and bullshit stopping me from putting my hands all over her.

"Skylar..." I run a hand through my hair and blow out a low exhale. "Just give me a second to get my head around this situation."

That brings the sparkle back to her eyes, and the sight makes my pulse thud even harder. How am I even fucking considering this? But equally, I don't know how I couldn't. Not when it comes to a girl as incredible as her.

"So, that's a *no* to getting changed?" Her teeth sink back into that plump lower lip, and all I want to do is tug on it. Better yet, I want to see those pink lips around my cock. Jesus, there's no guarantee this girl wants anything other than a bit of flirtation and attention, and here I am already imagining putting her on her knees.

"No." I let my gaze roam across her figure now. Relishing the way she shudders slightly, enjoying this long moment as I sip my whiskey and drink my fill of her at the same time. Allowing myself the act of properly appreciating such a sight. "You look way too fucking gorgeous for my sanity. Whoever all of this was meant for tonight—because I know it wasn't me—they're an idiot and don't deserve you."

Her lips twist into a way too cute and way too irresistible curve. "I'm glad someone got to appreciate it, at least."

She still looks hesitant, but any kind of smile on her, no matter how tiny, is sexy as hell.

"Trust me, I'm more than appreciative." I tip back another sip of my drink and swallow heavily. Unable to take my eyes off her. "Even though I shouldn't be."

I soak up the way her pupils blow out, and her lips hang a little parted. That small graze of our fingers might have felt electric before, but now it feels as though the air in my kitchen is crackling like a midwinter bonfire.

"Skylar..." I don't want to fucking say anything to disrupt this moment we're plowing toward, but I'd be the world's worst father if I didn't.

"I know." She nibbles on that bottom lip.

"What if he finds out? What then?"

"What if he didn't need to know?"

"But I'll know, and that's entirely the issue." I scratch my beard.

"Couldn't we both pretend? Since it's just this once..."

She thinks I only want her this one time. I *should* only want that, but there's a whole minefield of complications that come with admitting out loud how I really feel. That when it comes to this girl, I've had a lot of time to think about what I would do if I ever had the opportunity to have her.

None of which involved a fucking *one time only* situation.

However, she's right. As I take a long draw of my drink, mulling over what to say next, the writing is already on the wall.

"That snow isn't going to clear for a couple of days." My throat bobs, swallowing down the part of me demanding I find a way to stretch whatever this is beyond something as simple as being snowed in together. "Probably a good idea if it doesn't go any further than that."

"I think that's for the best."

"If we do this... we stick to the boundaries. As soon as this has to stop, it stops. Your friendship is more important and I'd fucking hate myself if..."

"You don't have to explain." Skylar dips her chin. "We're adults, right? We can play by some *rules*."

Oh, there are a whole lot of fucking games I'd like to play with this girl.

"Then, in that case." I tilt my glass at her. "Until the snow clears."

"Until the snow clears." Her sweet voice echoes mine.

Those bright blue eyes glint at me and my entire world slides sideways with the act of agreeing to this, even though there is no way in hell I should even be entertaining the idea.

"Thank you... for being so kind to me tonight." She breathes. "You've always made me feel so welcome here... you've always been a good friend."

That makes a gritty noise come out of me, and I place my glass down on the counter.

"Let's make one thing real clear, right fucking now." Leaning both hands on either side of her hips leaves me looming over her, so close I'm immediately wrapped up in her floral scent. "I don't want to be your *friend*, Skylar."

CHAPTER 10

I don't want to be your friend, Skylar.

Holy fuck.

I'm almost panting as the heat and masculinity of this man fills my senses. Lucas Rhodes is a solid wall consuming my vision and invading my space—along with my last remaining shred of sanity.

"I don't want to be your friend, or your friend's father, or anything else that makes it seem like I'm not over here fighting every urge to kiss the fuck outta you."

My eyes widen... entire body flushing.... pulse fluttering madly in my throat like it's trying to grow wings.

"You want that..." Suddenly, I feel so nervous. My big plan of seduction was all well and good until now we've reached that threshold and I'm instantly aware of how much older and more experienced this man is.

If this carries on, I don't want him to feel disappointed.

"I want a lot of things," he murmurs. Dark, hungry eyes fix on my mouth. "A lot of things I'm not supposed to wish for."

"It's Christmas... don't they say wishes come true?"

His lips twitch, and he reaches for the glass he set down just before.

"I'd say this is more like a fantasy wrapped up in a pretty pink bow."

God. This man is so hot. My cheeks feel like they might be on fire with his flirty words and roaming gaze.

"One you'd like to unwrap, I hope."

Luke lifts his drink, gives me a heated look, and then slides a thigh forward to part my knees. "You want to be unwrapped, sweetheart?"

Oh, god. I nearly whimper out loud.

Somehow, I manage a nod. Maybe I fumble out a *yes* but I'm not sure.

"Then tilt that pretty little head back for me and open your mouth."

My pussy clenches. The commanding tone in his voice is doing things to me I've only ever dreamed about.

So, of course, I do as he says, lifting my chin and dutifully opening.

Luke leans over me and very carefully pours a little whiskey from his glass onto my tongue. It's just enough to run slowly across my tastebuds, allowing me a taste, and that trickle of warmth feels like it floods everywhere, igniting my veins with desire.

"More?" His husky voice is so close.

I've never agreed to something more enthusiastically. Nodding quickly, I open my mouth again.

This time, the liquid doesn't hit my tongue like I'm expecting. It drips over my lower lip, and runs a trickle down my chin and neck.

"Fuck. I'm going to hell for this." I hear him groan, and then his mouth is on me. He fastens over my collarbone. Plush wet lips pair with scratches from his stubble as he sucks up the alcohol gathered there, followed by a moment that will remain forever ingrained in my memory, when he licks a scalding trail, tracing the line of whiskey up the column of my throat.

Up, up, up, until he reaches my mouth.

Luke hovers there, our lips only a frantic breath apart. Every inch of my skin feels like it's tingling with anticipation, and if I wasn't already hot for this man, with that one sinfully sexy move, he's just turned me into a complete slut, only for him.

"More?" That one word is so gravelly, so alluring. It makes heat pool low in my belly.

All I want to do is lose myself in this man. There's no guarantee Luke will even kiss me, yet right now I'm so lost in the moment, I'm not exactly sure that I care.

Somehow, I muster up the strength to nod. In all honesty, he can have whatever he wants, and I'll happily thank him for the opportunity. Multiple times over.

This time, his eyes roam all over me, as he brings that glass up to his mouth. Lucas Rhodes studies me like he's got all the time in the goddamn world, and I feel like I'm about to dissolve right here on the kitchen table.

"*Please.*" That single word gusts past my lips, shaky, so unbelievably turned on. Unwrap me, unravel me, whatever he wants, it's his.

He makes a rough noise, then takes a sip, all the while keeping my eyes entangled in his hooded gaze. Only, instead of swallowing, he leans over to cup the back of my head.

Those calloused fingers slide into my hair, and I gasp at the sensation of his heated touch.

That moment right there, is all it takes. He looms over me, so commanding and utterly handsome I feel like I'm living out every single fantasy moment I've ever created in my mind's eye.

And he spits into my mouth.

CHAPTER 11

Lucas

We should probably be talking about why this girl has ended up in my house, on my kitchen table, with my tongue running up her slender throat.

But right now, I get the impression that Skylar doesn't have any interest in talking.

Maybe that makes me an even worse person, but the fact that this beautiful girl has been left all alone on Christmas Eve makes me determined to show her just how much she is wanted.

Fuck talking. That can come later.

I spit the whiskey into her mouth, letting the liquid trickle down, and watch, captivated, as her blue eyes go wide and she gulps everything down. The quick swipe of her tongue to wet those damn plush lips of hers, has me going damn feral in an instant.

I fall on her with a noise that comes up from somewhere deep in my chest.

Sealing our lips together, it's hot and wet, and she tastes like I've completely lost my damn mind. Except, it's the single most incredible thing, feeling her softness and eagerness and the perfect way that she seems to fit against me.

We kiss like we've done this a thousand times before, and this is just one of many, many nights where I've been given the gift of the beautiful girl who hums into my mouth and makes the sweetest little whimpering noises.

"Want more?" I growl against her, meeting those panting breaths of hers in an effort to disguise my own.

Skylar whimpers, and I suck down on her tongue. Each second that our mouths keep searching and exploring, while my grip tightens in her hair, well, I'm ever closer to losing my damn mind.

"If that's what you want, I'm starting here." Reluctantly, I draw back, leaving her hastily wetting her lips, no doubt tasting the lingering hint of whiskey from both our mouths. This girl is something else entirely, looking gorgeous, flushed as all hell, and turned the fuck on. My fingers find the flimsy hem of her top, where the translucent material skims the high waistband on her skirt. "First, I'm starting with this slutty little tease of a thing. You think you can walk in here dressed like that without consequences?"

Seeing her little smile and flash of desire lighting her eyes feels like winning a goddamn buckle.

"Did I do something naughty?"

Oh, this girl wants to play *those* kinds of games.

"Extremely. Did you know I can see your bra?"

She feigns innocence, biting her cheek and shaking her head. As those pastel pink locks swing around her face, my dick is a steel bar inside my jeans.

I click my tongue, and she shivers. "You're not even sorry, are you? Parading around in here with your tits hanging out." I scold, hooking the fabric and sliding it up to sit over the swell of her breasts.

"I didn't mean to."

"I'm curious what you thought was going to happen. Did you think you wouldn't get caught being a little cock tease? Wandering around my ranch in those tiny cut-offs all summer? Creeping into the kitchen at this time of night wearing next to nothing."

"Sorry, I know I shouldn't have." Her chest rises and falls quicker as the backs of my fingers graze the softness of her cleavage.

Christ, it's taking everything in me to play this game and not tear each item of clothing off her in a frenzy.

"Well, you've landed yourself in big trouble now." Lowering my head, I take the top of her bra in my mouth and tug it down. Her breast pops free, pale, plump flesh, and rosy pink budded nipple right there, ready for the taking. "So much trouble." I quickly repeat the process on the other side.

"God, please." She lets out a soft moan as I run my nose and lips up the soft curve, until I reach the tightly furled bud.

"Bad girls don't get to ask for anything." I take the opportunity to blow gently on her nipple, and she squirms beautifully. Once again, I draw back, and it almost fucking kills me. Both her tits are squeezed and framed by the criss-crossed, sexy fucking black straps covering the front. Pressing her flesh and putting it on the most erotic display. Even though it pains me not to take her breast into my mouth—to suck down and hear her soft noises of pleasure like I goddamn want to—my next move is going to make it worth the fraction of extra time 'til I do so. To make this teasing and taunting worth it when I finally get to taste her nipples like I'm damn well salivating for.

Picking up the whiskey, I press the rim against the line where one of the black straps curves across her cleavage. Skylar quivers, breathing fast, as I let my eyes rake over the pair of breasts I should never have been given permission to see, let alone play with like this.

"Slutty little teases sit there quietly and take their punishment." Tipping the glass, I let a tiny trickle roll down her flesh, letting it run in a delicious track down the curve to cover her nipple, where it beads and hangs full and glistening.

Skylar lets out a soft, porny fucking noise. One that shoots straight to my balls and makes my cock jerk inside my jeans.

I repeat the process on the other side, coating her other nipple, before taking a moment to admire the sight. Both are glossy and have deepened to a more flushed shade. The vision of her, leaning back on her hands, tits bound up in that harness, with knees spread wide... that snaps my leash.

My mouth fastens over her breast. I'm swirling my tongue and sucking on her tight nipple, tasting the hit of whiskey and her scent while my hands wrap around and squeeze the outside of her soft thighs.

She tastes like everything fucking sweet and good and forbidden.

Because this girl is not meant for me, and yet I want to spend all night exploring all the ways I can make my son's best friend since they were both teenagers scream my name.

CHAPTER 12

Lucas

"Oh my god... *Luke...*"

I've officially lost my damn mind.

Skylar Addams is laid out like a feast before me, a girl who is far too young for an old cowboy like me, and I'm probably gonna have to renovate this fucking kitchen in the new year because there's no way I'll be able to do anything in here without getting hard at this memory.

I allow my teeth to graze her nipple and tug gently, drawing another moan and sultry cry of my name from Skylar's lips. A sound that I'm in danger of becoming addicted to.

"No, sweetheart. You've been very bad, wearing next to nothing covering your cunt. I don't think this even counts as a skirt, does it?" My palms push below the hem, sliding the leather up until I discover exactly what she's got hidden beneath that tiny piece of clothing.

If there was any chance this girl might just be my Christmas fantasy, that quick glance just confirmed everything. She's got sexy fucking garters on, her lush thighs reveal where they're wrapped up in soft black tights ending at the swell just below the hidden apex, and as I push the skirt all the way up, my brain short circuits.

"Fuck. You've been very, very bad, haven't you?"

Skylar whimpers, and her hips lift for me like the perfect goddamn dream she is so I can really look... so I can absolutely devour the sight that absolutely should not be for a man like me.

Yet we're here, and I'm staring at her almost exposed, perfect cunt.

"I think you forgot your panties, sweetheart." Voice low and husky; my eyes tip up to meet hers, and fuck me, she's going to be my utter ruin.

Skylar stares back at me with lust filling her expression, and just a hint of the way she bites her lip lets me know she's wondering what I'm thinking.

If it takes all fucking night, I'm going to show this girl just how magical she is. That she shouldn't be wasting her time with boys who can't appreciate every single stunning inch of her.

Allowing my gaze to drop back down, there's only the tiniest hint of ribbon and lace to match her bra covering this girl's pussy. It's virtually nothing; my teeth could tear that fragile fabric in a second, and yet it's a thousand times sexier than if she had nothing on at all.

"We're going to have to do something about this, too."

"Luke..." She sounds nervous. Hesitant.

"Sweetheart, this pussy is meant to be fucking worshipped... and I'm gonna ask you to trust me when I say that even if this is as far as we take things tonight, I need to eat your cunt 'til you fall apart. Preferably more than once."

She gasps and stammers as I lean closer. "It's—it's been a while."

"Then you obviously haven't had a real cowboy between

these thighs, so let me show you what you've been missing out on."

I'm beyond being able to resist anymore. Pulling up a chair, my eyes take in every detail, committing to memory this insanely perfect moment. Lowering my head, I grab her by the hips and tug. Skylar gasps as everything happens in quick succession.

With one palm, I press down on her sternum, firmly guiding her to lie back. Using the other, I hook her leg over my shoulder and sink forward, allowing my mouth to close over her.

The lace is so thin and fragile, it barely covers her pussy lips, and she tastes like a fucking dream come inexplicably to life right here in amongst the snow and the approaching midnight hour.

Skylar's back bows off the table, and she lets out a soft, sweet moan to match the flavor of her filling my senses.

Goddamn. It's addictive hearing how responsive her little noises are and feeling the way she trembles with every sweep of my tongue, nudging the material aside and exploring every delicate inch beneath my mouth.

Drawing back, I reach for my glass once more. This time, pouring a little over the scrap of barely there translucent thread.

Feeling the contrast, the way the cool of the whiskey caresses her skin, she shudders and whines. It's a series of delicious fucking sounds, and they morph and merge with the deep groan coming out of me when I dip my head, chasing the wetness. I can't get enough of this fucking goddess lying spread out for me as I suck and lick and attentively clean up every trace of the alcohol coating her pussy.

Stiffening my tongue, I massage over her clit, and feel the trembling start to roll through her body. She's close, so close, and I'm obsessed with the idea that this girl is going to shatter for me.

Somehow, unbelievably, I get to keep her for as long as this snow sticks around.

"That's it, beautiful..." I hover just over her, speaking against her drenched core. "Show me how bad you can be."

With that, I suck down on her clit through the soaked lace, and Skylar dissolves into her climax. The most addictive moans burst out of her, and she clamps her thighs around my head.

I didn't think tonight of all my lonely nights this year was going to be anything special, but goddamn, I think this girl might just be my own private miracle wrapped up in pastel pink and sexy as fuck lingerie.

CHAPTER 13

Skylar

My brain and body are strung out like a row of festoon lights, dangling somewhere between two different dimensions.

The cowboy between my thighs has a wicked tongue, and not just when it comes to his powers of dirty talk. He knows exactly how to unravel me and have my pussy crying out for him within seconds.

"Look at you, sweetheart. Dripping wet and a filthy little temptation lying here with these thighs wrapped round my head."

Luke's words are spoken right above my clit, and as he blows on the tiniest pair of panties I've ever dared to wear, my core clenches. I want him so badly. I want to know what it's like to be fucked by this man, even if it's only one time. I mean, I might cry if it's only tonight, but at least I've already had a sinful preview of how hard Lucas Rhodes can make me come.

Tonight feels like we've been able to suspend time and all the normal rules. So maybe, just maybe, this can go beyond the moment when this night officially ends.

"Please…" I murmur, gazing at him from beneath my

eyelashes. Hoping with bated breath that he's still invested in seeing this game through to the end.

"Still hungry for more?" As he runs his teeth across the fabric, they graze my pussy lips, and I swear there's so much heat and possessiveness coming off him, it sends sparks straight to my swollen clit.

I push myself up so that I'm sitting and nod my agreement. Did he just lick me so masterfully that I've forgotten how to talk? Luke straightens but remains seated between my knees, watching me closely. There's a sheen of *me* coating his stubbled beard and mouth that looks almost feral and makes my core clench. Eyes bouncing between my lips, my exposed tits, down to my skirt bunched around my waist, he's sinfully gorgeous.

"If you're hungry, then you can taste yourself first." He stands and swipes up the previously discarded glass of whiskey, swirling a sip around, as his gaze feasts on me splayed out and panting.

Oh god. I know what's coming next, and I'm such a slut for him. My mouth is already watering at the prospect.

Luke's eyes glimmer in the soft lighting, and he leans over me with a silent command in that dark stare.

Open.

My lips part on a soft whimpering noise, and this time I stick out my tongue. He lets the mix of saliva, whiskey, and my arousal all fall onto my mouth, and it sets my body alight. Cover me in fairy lights, and I'd make the perfect slutty Christmas decoration for this cowboy to use all night long.

I don't know how far this thing extends between us beyond physical desire and sex, but right now, I'm such a goner for him I don't give a shit. All I want is this cowboy's cock, I want him inside me, and I can't think straight about anything beyond letting him do whatever he wants.

Somehow, I just know, this is going to be the best damn sex of my entire life.

"Still not satisfied, are you?" He nibbles and sucks on my bottom lip, letting our mouths slide together, with a heady concoction of the scent and taste of *me* intermingling with the alcohol. "Is the taste of your cum on my tongue not enough to tame that hunger?"

"Just a little bit more, please... can I have that?" As he draws back, I flutter my eyelashes—entirely out of my depth and probably drunk on this man's cowboy pheromones alone—and reach out to rest my fingers over his belt. I'm hoping it comes across as sensual and confident, not like I'm so much younger and less experienced than him.

Luke makes a rough noise of approval in the back of his throat. "You're playing a dangerous game."

"If tonight is about wishes, then surely a little *game* wouldn't hurt?" He doesn't tell me no or shrug me off, and that's all I need. It's enough permission. I fumble with his buckle, then make quick work of his jeans. At least he's not stopping me from this next part, and that makes my stomach swoop in anticipation.

Luke's strong hands grip my thighs so hard I'm sure he's going to leave me with bruises to show where he's been. "Look at you. Making a mess all over my dining table, trying to tempt me into giving you what you came here looking for."

Biting down on my lower lip, I make sure to stare up at him as I shove his briefs down and allow the weight of his cock to bob freely.

"Just a little fun? No one has to find out." I'm nearly climbing out of my skin with how hot this is, waiting for him to give me the opportunity to take this further. The power dynamic between us is so heady, and even though he's in command, he's letting me be the one to take the lead with how far we go from here.

"Our little secret." He stares back at me with dark, glittering eyes before allowing his gaze to fall to the space between us.

I follow his silent command, as he instructs me to look my fill, and suck in a hum of pleasure at the sight I've been waiting for. Holy shit, my best friend's father has a cock worthy of worshiping twenty-four-seven. His thick length bobs between us. Veined and long and with a glistening bead at the head that makes my mouth water.

"I just want to show you... to let you know how good you made me feel." I wrap my fingers around him and stroke from root to tip. Loving the velvety feel and the way his dick swells in response to my touch. "Let me show you what you do to me."

He's so big, and we're already locked together here on the edge of the counter, that I guide him toward my slit easily. With one hand, I hook the lace to one side, and with the other, I stroke his tip through my slickness.

"*Mmmmfuck*, you're drenched. Who's all this for?" His chin dips, and our foreheads almost touch as we both watch the sight of where I repeat the motion over and over, dragging him through my pussy lips and up to circle over my clit.

"All for you."

A rumbling, sexy as fuck sound fills the air, leaving me shuddering with desire.

"So fucking wet. You're gonna have to be very careful... keep on doing that, and it might just slip in."

God. My entire core clenches. It's so naughty, so wrong, and the fact he's willingly playing this game with me is so hot I can hardly breathe.

"It's ok if it's only a little bit, isn't it? Especially if it's just our secret." My pulse thuds harder as I push the fat head of him down and notch him at my entrance. "No one needs to know. Just the tip."

"Sweetheart, you're going to get us in so much trouble," Luke grunts, spreading my thighs as wide as they can go. Allowing us to both see the evidence of this forbidden moment. Him coated in the sheen of my arousal and pressed up against the spot where it would take next to nothing for him to shove all the way inside.

"It's only this much. We can just play like this." I moan as I hold him tight against me, and he pushes forward just a fraction, fitting the broad head against my entrance.

"This pussy is so fucking greedy. You say you only want the tip, but really you're being a little tease, trying to tempt me deeper already." Luke's hips pulse, allowing his head to pulse in and out, thrusting agonizingly slow, so that barely an inch dips inside before he pulls back. I wedge my fingers there in a V shape to help guide him in place, to encourage just a fraction more of him to press inside my channel. The whole thing becomes even more erotic as each tiny movement is accompanied by a slick sound. One that proves exactly how soaking wet I am.

"It doesn't count if it's just this." My breathing picks up pace because, holy fuck, this man's cock is so insanely good. The feel of him stretching me is wiping my brain of any thoughts.

All I want is to lose myself in this man.

Luke shifts forward and then holds steady, his dick pushes inside, edging a little further, and I'm so close to begging him to slam all the way home. My pussy walls flutter and clench around him, and a dark noise leaves his chest.

My cowboy lifts one hand and pinches my chin, forcing me to look up at him. "You let me inside this pussy raw, and I'm going to have you stretched around my cock and leaking cum for as long as that snow sticks to the ground." He searches my gaze, eyes flickering between mine. "All games aside, better decide right now if that's what you want."

"Oh, god, I want that... more than you know." Yes, please, and thank you very fucking much. The picture he just painted makes my blood heat and sing. "I'm on birth control; I've been tested recently, and always normally use protection," I add hastily, feeling a little out of breath. Silently praying that if this man has any lingering doubts about going all the way through with this... well... hopefully that might convince him to shove all the way in deep.

He studies me. Something unreadable in his expression, and his jaw flexes. "Well, I haven't been with anyone without using a condom in... let's just say a long time. If that's enough for you to take me at my word, but I understand if it isn't."

God, he's so fucking hot. Brooding and powerful, not to mention the fact he's still fully clothed, while I'm in the sluttiest position where it feels even more filthy that I've got *almost* nothing on.

"Please, I need to feel you. I need you inside me." My Christmas wish is coming wrapped up in a big ol' bow of begging it would seem.

"You're going to watch." Luke guides my chin down, then hooks my thighs with both hands. All I can do is brace myself on my hands behind me as he manipulates my body into the exact position to sink deep. It's the hottest and filthiest sight, seeing us joined in the most carnal way.

"Look at your pretty little pussy taking every inch. See how well you take me."

We both stare, fixated on the place where his cock disappears into me. Where my body wraps and fits perfectly to stretch around all of him; with every mind-scrambling moment, he pushes forward on a long, wet glide.

"Luke..." I gasp. It's so full. He's everywhere, invading my body and mind on a level I'm not sure I'll recover from.

I've spent so many years of my life admiring this rugged man from afar, never wanting to let on just how much I've adored him for as long as I can remember knowing him.

"Goddamn, you're so fucking wet. So slippery. It's too good." Luke grits his teeth before he bottoms out, and we both let out a groan of pleasure.

He holds there for a second. The darkness in his eyes is completely hypnotic. They're black as the starless night outside, and as he pulls back, I bite down on my bottom lip.

Luke thrusts forward again, so commanding, so powerful, the force of him makes my breasts bounce, and the look on his face is entirely wild.

This man is going to turn my entire life on its head with this singular moment, I can feel it.

Sliding out again, I'm so slick and turned on, he draws back to just the tip. With a rough noise, his fingers grip my flesh and he thrusts home. Again and again.

"Holy fuck." His voice is so gritty and sexy. I'm immediately lost in how insanely pleasurable it feels to be with him.

Not to mention how every single detail of this moment is unfathomably hot.

My best friend's father pounds into me while I'm spread out on the dining table we've sat at for countless meals together. A place so familiar it might as well be my own kitchen.

Nothing will ever be the same after this, but I have no fucking regrets. This is everything I've wanted for so long and never thought could ever be a possibility.

"Oh god. Oh god." As Luke keeps thrusting forward, tension starts to whirl and build, and pleasure starts to build from my toes like a whirlwind intent on sweeping me away.

"Jesus. You're gripping me so tight. It's too fucking good."

"I'm so close." The moan I let out is loud and desperate.

"You're gonna let me inside you all night." Strong fingers sink into my softness, holding me exactly where he wants me to keep hitting a spot that makes my eyes roll back in my head.

"Please. *Please.*"

"Where do you want me to come?" He grits his teeth. We're both dangling on the edge as his thrusts start to get jerkier and sloppier, just how fucking good this feels consumes the two of us all at once.

"Inside." I gasp, barely holding on.

"You want me to fill this pretty little cunt up?" Luke grinds out the words with each punishing thrust.

"Yes. Come inside me." My words are hardly more than a whimper. "Oh god. I want to feel it."

Letting out a dark noise, that's when he seeks out my clit.

I simply dissolve. My pussy clamps down so hard I think I see stars and blank spots behind my eyelids as a powerful climax tears through me.

"Jesus. Fuck. *Fuck.* I'm gonna fill you over and over."

Luke's hips jerk in an unsteady rhythm, and as my orgasm is still rolling through, my pussy still rippling and gripping him, I feel it. The length of him swells, and he makes a rough noise, burying himself deep.

His cock throbs and spills inside me, and I'm pretty sure there are moans coming out of me at how good it feels.

Holy shit, the feeling of him unloading, pulsing inside is like nothing else.

Nothing is going to compare to this.

As we both remain there, joined together, panting and attempting to catch our breath, I suspect that I've just allowed part of my foolish little heart to stay right here when I leave this place.

CHAPTER 14

Lucas

"Don't act like it's the end of the world, Tessie-girl."

She nudges my shoulder and nibbles the collar of my jacket with a snort as I give her breakfast.

We're all creatures of routine, and the horses have all looked at me with big, dewy eyes as if I have three heads for being out here so early this morning.

It's still dark out, the freezing air crisp, and I've left a gorgeous girl sleeping in my bed after the hottest night of my life.

However, a ranch doesn't wait, or give a shit about my sex life—or lack thereof the majority of the time—so I'm rushing around with a flashlight in the dark and trudging through snow.

All so I can get back to her at the earliest opportunity.

Munching noises and gentle huffing sounds follow me as I check on all the stalls and make sure everyone is warm and comfortable after last night's storm.

The familiar scent of wood, leather, and hay surrounds me. Smells that feel embedded in my very bones after so many years running this ranch. There are plenty of jobs I'll have to get to later today, but mucking out stalls can wait.

I've got somewhere else I need to be.

My phone vibrates in my coat pocket, and I scrunch my brows as I dig it out. It doesn't matter that it's Christmas morning; I don't know anyone who would be messaging me at this time of the day.

BRAD:
> Merry Christmas, old man.

GUILT IMMEDIATELY FLOODS me at the sight of Brad's name. Does my son have fucking sixth sense or what?

> You're up early.

> Oh, good. You're as pleasant over text as you are in person at this time of day.

> Repeat after me... "Merry Christmas, my son, the light of my life. I hope you and Flinn have a wonderful day and enjoy the thousands of dollars I just deposited in your bank account."

> Go on. Try it.

> Fuck off.

> Merry Christmas.

> There we go.

> Not so hard, was it?

> Doesn't answer my question. Why are you texting me at this time of the morning?

BOUQUETS & BUCKLES

> Jesus. I'll warn Sky you're in particularly good spirits for Christmas Day.

> In case it's escaped your notice, ranch life has ruined mornings for both me and Flinn.

> Even when it's a day off, we can't enjoy sleeping in anymore.

More dots bounce on the screen.

> Please, can you at least not be all 'grumpy asshole' today.

> Treat my best friend nicely... you know, be good to her when she gets up.

Oh. I've got plans to treat her extremely well, but my son doesn't need to know any of that.

I readjust my hat with my free hand, staring at my phone glowing in the dark, contemplating what to write in reply. God, I feel like no matter what I say, it'll sound suspiciously like I know exactly how Skylar Addams feels when she grips my cock so hard I nearly lose my goddamn mind. If I try to say anything, it'll reveal that I know the exact way her eyes roll back and how her little moans sound as she falls apart.

I figure saying less is always going to be the best option.

> Of course.

> Love you, Dad.

> Give the horses a big hug for me.

I'm about to tuck my phone away when I see more dots bouncing.

> Keep an eye on Sky, would you?

> She might say she's doing ok, but she found out her piece of shit boyfriend was cheating on her last night.

My hand scrubs over my jaw as I see my son's next messages arrive. Texts that leave me with a hundred conflicting emotions about who my son thinks I am as a good father, and who I am underneath as the man who wants to savor every second I have left in secret with this girl.

Not to mention the extreme need I'm battling... the urge to go beat the hell out of whoever this asshole is. The mere sight of those words on screen has me seeing red.

Except, Brad's next message arrives and reminds me that I don't need to go over there and acquaint my fist with the fucker's jaw. Because I have her.

I have her.

Even if it's just temporarily.

> Thanks for being there when I couldn't be.

> I'm just glad she's safe with you.

CHAPTER 15

My body runs white hot, with a cascade of liquid pleasure flowing through my heavy limbs.

There's a weight draped over my body, pinning me hard to the mattress, and as I stir, the scents of *Lucas Rhodes* and the soft cocoon of his sheets gradually come into sharper focus.

Followed by the glide of his tongue.

His hot mouth is on my pussy, working me, guiding me into yet another climax.

I don't know when we finally drifted to sleep, but after a marathon of sex, he's still not satisfied. Taking his time to lick and suck and drive me into a bank of rainbow clouds, flying somewhere high out of my body.

My fingers reach down and sink into his hair, holding him in place against my pussy, and a sigh of pleasure escapes into the darkness of his bedroom.

Fuck, this cowboy is my every fantasy and dirty fascination come to life. He's so skilled with his tongue, building my coiled desire up before easing back and letting me sink even deeper into how fucking incredible this feels.

Luke isn't doing this to try and get me off in a hurry like some guys I've been with in the past might do; he's nestled himself between my thighs and seems like he's intent on staying there.

"You're gonna have me addicted, Mr. Rhodes." My voice is raspy with sleep, and possibly after screaming his name over and over, as I roll my hips and tighten my fingers in his hair.

He grunts. A delicious, hungry noise, sucking and nibbling on my pussy lips. "Fuck... Christmas or not, today can fuck right off... neither of us are leaving this bed for the rest of the day."

A moan gets dragged out of me when he doubles down and pushes his tongue inside. "Mmm. Oh god," I whimper. Yes, please, I'll gladly dissolve into orgasm after orgasm without coming up for air. If his mouth, fingers, or cock are involved, that's more than enough to satisfy my needs.

"So pretty when your legs shake for me." He speaks against my sensitive bundle of nerves, and I want him to keep circling with that perfect rhythm. I'm a swollen, slick mess after everything we've done since last night.

"Luke... I can't... not again." I moan, but the man is relentless.

"Be my perfect little slut and soak my face." Those wicked words are followed by him sucking down on my clit, making my back bow up off the bed as my orgasm rushes in from where it has been hovering in the wings, waiting for my mind to wake up.

The intensity and suddenness surprises me, showcasing just how long he's been playing with my body while I've been asleep. How insanely hot that is, how naughty, well, the sensation roars through my blood, and I'm making all sorts of wanton noises while chanting his name over and over.

If I wasn't already dangerously close to falling head over heels for this man, I think he might have just sealed my fate.

How will I ever top this? How will I ever find anything to compare to how good it feels, inexplicably so, with a cowboy twice my age?

Luke doesn't stop, expertly flipping my body so that he can drive into me from behind. This time he fucks me fast, our bodies line up perfectly at this angle and he hits a spot deep inside that makes me feel delirious with pleasure. I'm spun out of my head entirely by his forceful thrusts, and powerful body braced over the top of me.

"Fuck, you're the sweetest thing. Moaning my name and coming for me. You're gonna have me addicted to your cunt." His voice is hot at my ear, and it makes my climax drag out or keep building, I'm not sure which anymore. But all I know is that I'm tightening around him again, and he curses, feeling the way I can't help but respond. To him, to his words, to the way he spears into me, to the dragging sensation of his thickness gliding in and out of my channel.

"God... Luke... "

"You want me to fuck you full, sweetheart? Have my cum dripping out of you?"

"Yes. *Yes.*" I dissolve under the weight of his filthiness.

His hand snakes around to find my clit, and it only takes a couple of firm circles; that deft touch picks me up and washes me over the edge. Luke follows me. His hips falter, and his cock throbs and jerks deep inside my pussy as he grunts out his release.

It's so fucking sexy hearing the way he falls apart above me, and even though my pulse races blindly with desire, I feel my heart melt more than a little.

His mouth roams across my shoulders in a sanity-stealing glide of wet kisses.

"Hell, you squeeze my cock like a dream." Luke rumbles at

my ear, not making any attempt to move. God, I can't get over how incredible it feels to be filled by this man.

"How does a bath sound?"

Holy shit, did I just squeak out loud?

"So, that's a yes?"

Reluctantly, we untangle ourselves, and I squirm around to face my cowboy, who leans over my body, caging me in with his impossibly broad arms.

"I forgot you have a bathtub. I miss having one since I moved out of home." I peek up at him, still floating around somewhere on blissed-out waves. "Yes. A *very* enthusiastic yes, but on one condition."

He brushes strands of hair away from my face and raises one eyebrow. A silent question.

"You have to join me, cowboy."

Luke blows out a chuckle and drops his head against my chest. "I'm trying my damnedest to be giving you some rest, Skylar. Not trying to get inside you at every opportunity."

"Can I be honest, and you promise not to laugh?" I just want to hold him here, pressed against me, weighing me down against the mattress.

His lips brush my collarbone as he speaks against my skin. "Anytime. You know me."

I bite my lip. Trying to find the courage to ask for what I want, when eventually, I just blurt it out. "I'm a cuddler… after sex… and since we've, well, you know *a lot*… it's feeling extra intense for me right now."

Luke nuzzles my neck and runs his nose down to my cleavage. "Sounds like a dream. A hot as fuck girl who can't keep her hands off me. What's not to get excited about in that scenario?"

I try not to give away with the look on my face or the immediate tension that fills my limbs, the number of guys—my asshole ex included—who would never give me that kind of simple affection afterward.

The man pinning me to the bed senses it all the same.

"Don't even answer that question because I don't need to spend the next hour talking myself out of going over there and sorting that piece of shit out."

I can't help but laugh. Luke picks me up off the bed, sets me on my feet, then herds me toward the bathroom, as if I've got any intention or interest in going anywhere else. Before long, we're both soaking in divine steaming water, with him at my back and his big palms running soap leisurely over my arms, my stomach, and my breasts.

He's not trying to start anything, but treats me to a constant stream of touches that make my bones dissolve with bliss.

At this point, I'm willfully ignoring the fact my heart has formed a little puddle of besotted happiness, too.

CHAPTER 16

I could die a contented man if I never have to leave this damn bathtub.

The sweetest, most gorgeous woman I've ever met is wrapped against my chest, and time feels like it has gone into hibernation while we've been soaking in here together.

"Don't you need to go take care of the horses this morning?" Skylar plays her fingers over my forearm, sending tiny sparks swirling beneath my skin as she does so.

"Already done."

"What? When?" She tries to tilt her head around to look at me.

"Earlier... I didn't want to wake you."

"Oh my god. I could have at least come and helped out, you know."

I shake my head ruefully, quietly laughing to myself at how pouty she sounds. "Sweetheart, it's freezing outside, and everything is buried under three feet of snow. I've done that routine what feels like a million times, it's easy for me. The fact I could climb back into bed and have you soft and warm and moaning my name... now that's the best gift you could give me."

Skylar makes a little noise, part protest and part embarrassment. Fuck, she's so cute, the way she starts to squirm.

"I still can't believe this is real." Her voice is quiet.

How much do I tell her?

How much do I dare admit?

"Why wouldn't it be?" My hands roam freely because there's every chance I'm more than addicted to the way her delicate skin feels beneath my rough palms.

"I didn't think *Lucas Rhodes* would ever notice someone like me."

Fucking hell. If only this girl knew...

"I've always noticed you," I speak against her hair. Sitting like this, it's impossible to ignore the way she fits so perfectly, nestled into my chest.

"Really?"

"Look... not when you were younger, of course. Not in *that* kind of way back then." I'm quick to add, while painfully aware of the fact I now have my son's best friend naked in my bath.

She can't help but giggle a little. "It would be way too easy to tease you about that right now."

Pinching her thigh makes her jump and let out another laugh. The kind of sound that roams straight through my chest, breaking through years of self-imposed guards and walls that have existed there for too damn long along the way.

"Joke all you like, sweetheart, but let's just make it abundantly clear. I never looked at you that way when you were younger. The reason I always noticed *you* was because Brad was able to be himself around you."

I rest my lips against her pink hair, inhaling deep lungfuls of her scent. Shampoo and soap and sweetness that is so undeniably Skylar.

"You know, Brad came out to me when he was about twelve,

I think... he asked me if I liked boys as much as I liked girls. If I ever had trouble choosing between the two. Which at the time he asked was outta left field, but we were right in the middle of grooming the horses together, so all we did was chat about it while we worked, and he was just so certain. As a parent, there wasn't ever a doubt in my mind that he was bisexual. It's just who Brad is. But I know not every person in the world can see past their own prejudices and bullshit. So I always worried about him. I always worried about who he was hanging out with... and yet, I always knew if the two of you were together, he would be ok."

A wistful sigh comes out of her. "I don't want to hurt him, and I don't want to do anything to mess up your relationship with him either."

"I know you never would." This is also why I know this girl will never jeopardize their closeness or friendship, no matter how good it might feel to temporarily indulge in whatever this is together. "It made me sleep better at night knowing he had you as a friend, Skylar."

"You're a good dad, you know. The best."

I groan. "Can you maybe not remind me about that while I've got you naked." Right now, I definitely don't feel particularly responsible in the father-figure department.

Her silent laughter rolls through her body, making her shake a little against my chest.

"Ok, funny girl, laugh all you like. I've told you when I first noticed you." Dropping my head down, I brush my lips up the side of her neck. "Now you have to confess... when did you first notice me?"

She makes a sinful little noise as my lips explore the side of her throat, and even though Skylar arches her neck to give me more access, her hands fly up to cover her face.

"Ohhhh... it's like that, is it?" I tease.

Skylar continues to squirm.

I'm enjoying this much more than I should. My dick is, too.

"You can't torture me on Christmas. That's not fair." She whines.

"I think I can. Maybe denying you any more orgasms might work?" My fingers play over her inner thighs, taunting as I dip close to her pussy, without making any contact.

Skylar's hips try to chase my touch, and I have to stifle a groan. All I want to do is lift her up and settle her back down over my cock, but we both need to actually leave this bathroom and eat something, considering we've done nothing but fuck since last night.

"I can't remember a time when I didn't have hearts in my eyes whenever I saw you." She twists so that she can meet my gaze, tilting her chin to look up at me. "How you didn't see that, I'll never know."

"You must have been pretty good at hiding these baby blues," I murmur. Wondering how, in all those years, I never noticed her looking at me like that.

"I would have been nothing more than a silly little girl to your eyes."

Bringing one hand up out of the water, I tuck her hair behind her ear and brush wet fingers along the softness of her cheek. Once again, I take my time to study her, to look my fill, and really, truly savor looking. To commit to memory the swirling, endless, azure blue-filled orbs with tiny flecks of silver.

"Sweetheart, even if I had noticed back then, it wasn't my place to look at you..." I brush my thumb along her bottom lip. "But now? I'm selfish and greedy, and I'm gonna want you naked until that snow clears so I can look at you all I like. How does that sound?"

Her teeth catch her bottom lip, and she looks like a goddamn dream.

"As long as I get to do the same with you, cowboy."

CHAPTER 17

A sultry moan drops out of Skylar.

"Oh my god."

She squeezes her eyes closed, and I have to fight the urge to toss our plates aside and give in to the perpetual need to have my mouth on her again.

"This... hands down... is the best Christmas lunch I've ever had." She says through a mouthful.

Taking another big bite of the grilled cheese, she's a gorgeous sight, bundled up in a blanket in front of my fireplace in the lounge. Hair damp and skin glowing after the bath. I got my wish to keep her naked, but Skylar reluctantly agreed to let me throw on some sweats while I made us a meal.

"I don't believe that for a second." Biting into my own, the savory hit of melted cheese and caramelized edges of the bread do taste damn good. "But I will say, there's an art to grilled cheese, I don't give a shit what anyone thinks. You gotta do it properly. Crisp that motherfucker a little, ya know?"

Skylar chews quietly, then gestures at the sight beside us where we've camped out on the floor for this impromptu picnic.

"The tree looks so pretty. I didn't think I'd want to see a

single bauble or scrap of tinsel after the past few weeks of being neck-deep in making everyone else's Christmas look gorgeous, but I'm kinda glad to get to see some cute decorations and lights."

I clear my throat because, if anything, the sight I'm looking at right here before me with her pink hair and gorgeous smile is a thousand times better than that goddamn tree.

"It's all Brad's doing. Can't say I've contributed anything really."

"Bet you still chopped the tree down for him, though, just like you do every year?"

Giving her a wry smile, I reach forward to brush a crumb off the corner of her lips with my thumb.

"Shh, sweetheart. Don't give away all my secrets. If I had it my way, I'd have nothing at all... I've never been much into Christmas, to be honest. Brad however..."

The prettiest girl in the entire fucking world tips her head back and laughs, earning her a glare.

"What?" I huff.

Skylar rolls her lips together, shaking her head. "I'm not really sure I can be bothered with it either... all the day usually does is remind me of being single, and it's just another day where everything seems to be about buying shit they don't need and spending time with people they don't want to be around."

Ain't that the fucking truth.

"So my stupid little grilled cheese and a tree that my son insisted on inserting in my house and decorating—that's enough Christmas spirit for you?"

She hums while breaking off a corner, letting the melted cheese stretch out between the pieces with a smile that I don't deserve to be enjoying so much.

"Look, I'm nothing but a hazard in the kitchen. Anyone who can make me a meal that tastes *this* good is a saint in my eyes."

"Do you not cook for yourself?" My brows crease.

"No, I'm either too tired, too busy, or find it easier to get takeout." She mulls over a mouthful, and then her blue eyes roll at me. "Don't give me the *dad* look of judgment either."

"Well, what do you expect me to say? You're not taking care of yourself."

"I've never been any good at cooking, and it's just so hard when your business is new." Skylar brushes some additional crumbs from the corner of her mouth with a thumb.

I get it. I really do. There have been plenty of times on this ranch when work or the horses have come first, and my own needs a distant second. Even so, it chafes to know this girl has been potentially working herself to the bone with no one there to take care of her.

"No one's been there to help you?" I want to fucking punch whoever she's been allowing in her life. Clearly, the asshole she was with didn't know shit about how to keep such a perfect girl.

His loss.

My gain.

She takes another mouthful, avoiding my eyes as she chews. The fireplace pops and hisses to fill the silence.

"Turns out I let the wrong kind of asshole into my life, and I should have listened to Brad a long time ago." She eventually admits. "But, is it ok if we don't talk about that?"

"Fine by me, I probably shouldn't be threatening to break anyone's jaw, seeing as it's Christmas and all."

Skylar gives me a small smile.

"Cooking for me and defending my honor. Where have you been all my life, cowboy?"

I know she's teasing, but hell, if it doesn't make me wonder the same thing. How the fuck has this girl been in my life all these years, yet only now are we discovering this spark between us?

Especially when I know there's only a matter of time until that snow is cleared and she's gone again.

"You're letting me help with the horses tomorrow. End of story." Skylar drops her Kindle into her lap and pouts at me when I walk back into the lounge.

I've been out getting all the basic shit done down in the stables but insisted that Skylar didn't need to help me.

Besides, I'd have never gotten anything done anywhere near as quickly if she'd been there alongside me. Not because she's incapable, but because I wouldn't have been able to keep my hands off her.

I tug my hat off my head and run my fingers through my hair.

"Ahh, but that means putting clothes on, and I much prefer the idea of coming back in from the cold to find you naked on my couch, sweetheart." I lean a shoulder against the wall and touch my tongue to the front of my teeth, eating up the way she flushes perfectly under my words.

"I'm serious." She tugs the blanket tighter around her shoulders, and I fucking love that she's stayed right here, without anything on, settled in front of my fire all afternoon.

"Ok, fine, you can come scoop horse shit to your heart's content tomorrow. Does that make you happy?"

"Very. Thank you." She gives me a satisfied little smirk and then picks up what she was reading. Only, as I go about stripping out of my jacket and boots, I feel her eyes straying my way.

"Good book?" Once I've hung everything up, I cross the room and bank the fire with more wood. Purposely taking my time.

"Mmhm." She sinks her teeth into the plump curve of her lower lip, trying extremely hard to keep her eyes focused on the screen.

"Not too boring for you, I hope? Being stuck in here all day with only a book to keep you occupied."

I've got plans to make this much more interesting.

"Nope, it's kinda perfect." Her tongue darts out to wet her lips. Pink spots deepen, high on her cheeks, and fuck, she looks so sexy.

"You're welcome to put a movie on... if you prefer?"

"I don't mind, it's your house. What do you want?"

"Me? I like the idea of getting cozy right there beside you with a book. As long as that doesn't sound too *old and boring* to you?" Crossing to the couch, I'm shit stirring after what I heard Brad say to her on the phone last night. Except if I'm truthful, beneath the teasing, there is a tiny part of me who is still a little unsure what this girl even sees, or wants, with someone like me.

Skylar shifts over, making room for me to wedge myself in the corner of the L-shaped couch as I swipe up a book I've had sitting on the side table here for months, yet my eyes are usually too heavy to manage reading more than a couple of pages at a time.

"Honestly... after how crazy the last few weeks have been at my shop, it actually feels amazing to have the luxury of time and quiet and to not have to talk to anyone."

Oh, I can definitely do *not talking*.

"Come here." My dream girl, whom I cannot keep, nestles herself against my side, with her head on my chest and hand holding her Kindle braced against my stomach. I prop my own book up on my chest, but in all honesty, I'm not focusing on a single fucking word.

My other arm snakes over her waist, palm covering her hip. It's too tempting to see just how silky and wet she might be between those thighs.

As we lie there together, I feel her shift a little beneath my fingers. That's the moment her breathing shallows, and I can't help myself. Slipping my hand between the layers of blanket, I trace the lush curve of her stomach down, down, down until I find the exact place where I want to explore.

Skylar's breath sucks in with a quiet gasp as my fingers dip into her pussy and find exactly what I'm looking for.

Discovering how absolutely drenched she is.

"Luke..." She makes a tiny moaning sound that makes my rapidly hardening cock kick inside my jeans. Turning her head into my chest, teeth graze the front of my shirt.

"Are you sore?" I stroke gently, running my fingers through the velvety feel of her. The slippery evidence of how turned on the girl in my arms is, coats my fingers.

"No." Her hips lift and adjust, giving me easier access. "I can't stop thinking about you being inside me again."

That makes me more feral for her than I have any right to be.

"Keep reading. If you can be a good girl and let me play with you, without coming, I'll give you exactly what you want."

CHAPTER 18

"Can you be good and do that for me?"

The glide of Luke's fingers against my clit, rubbing through my soaking wet pussy is all I can focus on.

"I don't know." My whimper catches in my throat as he strokes and fondles me so damn leisurely, almost like this is completely normal. As if we lie here on this couch wrapped together like this every night, while he teases my pussy until my thighs shake.

How much I want that... how much every detail of that scenario swirls in my mind as something I dearly wish could be true, shocks me.

I mean, I know how deeply besotted I've always been with this man. Except all of those years he was simply a fantasy, a young girl's infatuated desire with a much older and sinfully attractive cowboy.

This feeling right here, catches me by surprise, that I might want this to be something more than just sex and being able to finally live out the longing I'd had in my head for so many years.

"*Hmm.* I think you can. Especially if you want to have me

inside you all night." Luke's deep voice vibrates through his thick chest and into me, along with the ripples of pleasure each time he lingers over my clit, before easing away, continuing to torture me the whole time.

I'm panting within minutes. Quivering for him. Tiny, slutty, begging noises burst out of me. The climax threatening to take over, that I so desperately want to chase, hovers close and then ebbs time and time again. Somewhere along the way, my Kindle has slipped from my fingers, and all I'm capable of is clutching onto his soft shirt.

"Please. Luke, I can't take any more." A shudder rolls through me, and white sparks dance behind my eyelids as I get lost in how insanely good it feels to allow him command over my body.

"This might just be my favorite way to spend the holidays," he murmurs wickedly. Using two fingers to curl inside me, he presses forward to gather up more of my slickness, then spreads it up and over my clit with a slide of his touch that is just enough to wind me tighter, but nowhere near enough to get me off. "Feel how goddamn drenched you are for this."

There is every chance I'm flying out of my head by this point. I've never had anyone treat me like this before, and my entire body feels like a sparking livewire.

My skin is overheated, and my breasts ache, and it takes everything not to start damn well humping his hand.

"Oh god. Please." Begging is my only currency.

"You want to come, sweetheart?"

"Yes," I whimper, digging my fingernails into his shirt. I want him naked, too, like he promised me.

"Get up here." His fingers drag out of my pussy, leaving an obscenely slick trail across my stomach. Slipping out from under the warmth of the blanket, I allow him to guide me up over his chest.

I'm not even sure I can support my own body weight; every limb feels so heavy with pleasure.

A gasp slips out of me as he makes his intentions clear.

I was expecting us to be fucking, but it seems Luke has other ideas. His big hands wrap around my waist, strong fingers digging into the softness of my curves, and he firmly holds me still while sinking lower down the couch.

Holy shit.

There's a hunger in his eyes that turns me upside down and inside out as I realize he's positioning me over his mouth. That look, right there, makes my blood sizzle with anticipation, but it feels so insane. We're doing this, right here, out in the open, and even though I know that no one could possibly see anything, there's enough risk that it turns up the intensity of this moment to scalding proportions.

"No hovering. Full weight. Sit your pretty little pussy right where I want." He licks up the swell of my inner thigh. The exact place where I know I'm coated in wetness from being so turned on and so out of control when it comes to this man.

"But—" I can't help it. I want this, and I want him, yet I'm also so easily stuck inside my own head with doubt.

"Full." *Nip.* "Body." *Lick.* "Weight." *Suck.*

"Oh fuck. Oh fuck." My hands fly to his hair. Sinking into the unruly dark strands, threading through the flashes of silver, tangling with that hot as fuck white streak I've longed to reach out for.

Luke forces me to sink down onto him, and his mouth closes over my pussy, leaving me moaning out loud. I'm grinding down on him immediately because it feels so incredible. After all his teasing and torturing, I'm strung tight and know I'll hurtle over the edge of this cliff almost straight away.

He doesn't waver this time. This man is on a mission to make me shatter, and as his tongue pushes into my pussy I'm moaning, cursing, chanting his name. I tug his hair so hard it must be painful, but that sting against his scalp only seems to spur him on.

That's when he shifts me slightly, fingers digging into my hips so hard they might surely bruise, and he locks me in a dangerously dark stare. He sucks down on my clit so hard my back bows, and the wave breaks right on top of me. Leaving me shaking and crying out.

Hopefully *not* telling him that I'm in love with him, or something equally ridiculous.

With each subsequent moment he makes me shatter, I'm only falling deeper into whatever this is. The sensations keep growing more and more intense, and I don't know how I'm going to cope when it all has to stop.

"Oh my god. I need you inside." My heart thunders in my throat. Blood tingling and sparks flying through each limb form a pulsating rhythm.

"You want my cock?" he speaks against my pussy, and I nearly jerk away with how overstimulated I am.

"I do. Please. I've been so horny for you all day." The desperate words burst out of me.

"Well, I'm nowhere near done here. So, if you want my dick in your mouth, you better turn around for me."

"Holy shit."

There's a devious look in his eyes, and glistening evidence of my wetness all over his mouth and beard.

"Problem?" He steals my breath as he holds my gaze and runs his tongue in a long line to lap at my pussy.

"Right here?" My eyes flicker around the room. I'm intensely aware of how naked I am, perched over his face.

"My house. My rules. If I want the sweetest damn pussy I've ever had soaking me right here, that's how it's going to be."

A tiny smile tugs at my lips. "You're naughty, Mr. Rhodes."

CHAPTER 19

"*I'm naughty?* Says the girl who walked in here wearing nothing but a bra and a pathetic excuse for panties last night. Now suck my dick while I eat your cunt 'til you can't argue with me anymore."

Luke tumbles me down, and in my post-orgasm haze, I'm entirely boneless, allowing him to position me in the sluttiest way possible. Completely naked, on hands and knees over the top of him, with his bulging erection pressing against the front of his jeans, right there in my face.

God. How I want to show this man exactly how much I enjoy having his dick in my mouth.

In between all our midnight fucking, I had a few opportunities to run my tongue over his length, to lick, to wrap my lips around him briefly. This moment right here is the first time I'll properly get to suck his cock, and I'm practically salivating for him.

Luke lets me kneel over his chest while I work his jeans and briefs in order to take him out. As soon as his cock bobs free, the second my hungry fingers have succeeded in their quest, he strikes. Dragging me back up over his mouth, he tips me forward in order to begin running his tongue all over me again. Building me back up in a way that I didn't know was even possible for my body twenty-four hours ago.

My mind goes blank, pleasure washes through me, and my toes curl.

"Oh fuck." I'm the horniest girl alive for this man. "How are you so good? Everything feels so good with you." My words are part moan, part sob, as I allow my tongue to run the length of him, from root to tip, sloppy and desperate licks that feel incredible against his thickening shaft.

Beneath me, I feel him groan against my pussy, and I take that as my invitation to do it again and again. Drawing as many of those delicious noises as possible out of the cowboy with his head between my thighs.

I'm getting close, the wave starts to build, and the intensity of pleasure winding a path straight through me sends me to a place where nothing exists except trying to please Lucas Rhodes.

I allow a long trail of spit to fall from my lips and watch on in fascination as his dick jerks in response.

Luke makes a muffled noise against my pussy, tightening his hold on my hips. "*Ffffuck.*"

"Do you like that, Mr. Rhodes?" I'm not sure what has come over me, but there's a reckless devil at the helm now, and she wants to see this man lose control.

"Christ." He grunts and drags his teeth across my sensitive flesh. I don't miss the way his tip glistens and length throbs in response to me calling him that. "If you can still talk, that's a problem. Be a good girl and give me one more, then I'm going to fill you with my cock all night."

Luke shoves his tongue inside me and I nearly fall apart right then and there. He's relentless, devouring me, and I do my best to match his pace, mirroring his actions. Swirling my tongue over the fat head of him before sucking down.

His dick tastes masculine and feels velvety, filling my mouth. That slight saltiness of pre-cum slides across my tongue, and everything about him is perfect. I can take him so much deeper at this angle, letting him in with ease. It's so fucking hot, like this, on his couch. The fact he's been so desperate to have me, that he's still fully clothed and I'm naked... well, that feels powerful somehow.

Like this man would gladly worship me and tend to my needs and my needs alone.

As I start to tremble and feel that rush of pleasure build higher and higher, I'm moaning around his length. His heat and scent fill my senses, and when he works me with two fingers along with his tongue, that does me in. My orgasm hits with a rolling force. I'm a mess of drool, bobbing up and down, making all sorts of desperate, panting noises.

"Fuck, you're so perfect." In between the buzzing in my ears and the thundering pulse in my neck, I'm being manhandled once more.

Luke flips us so that he's sitting up and has me in his lap. I'm dimly aware that my arms hook to drape around his neck while letting him maneuver my body, and I don't fucking care.

He can have whatever he wants.

"*Mmmmfuck.* Don't tempt me with wanting to keep you, sweetheart." He sinks our mouths together at the same time as impaling me on his fat cock. I'm such a wet and swollen mess after having him eat me until I can't even think straight that he slides in so fucking deep, stretching me perfectly around him.

All I can do is cling to his neck and whimper into his mouth. Everything turns to bright sparks and unfathomable pleasure. The material of his shirt drags against my hard nipples, and my clit brushes up against his lower stomach.

"God. You're so tight. So fucking perfect." He pinches my bottom lip between his teeth, fucking up into me, while my body burns hot and blazing for him. "Give me those tits."

With calloused, big palms, he cups my breasts. Pinching and squeezing my nipples while dipping his head to suck and swirl his tongue everywhere.

My fingers dig into his unruly hair, and I keep clinging to him. Holding him there with my head dropped back and eyes squeezed shut.

"Oh god. Oh god." I can feel it. The liquid feeling starts to flow up from my toes, and it's so good but so much, and I don't know how much more of this I can take.

"Milk my cock. That's it. Just like that." Luke grunts against my breasts, still lavishing them with attention in a way that feels like he knows every single key to unraveling my body.

"I'm gonna have you wrapped around me until morning. I don't wanna stop fucking you, it feels too good to stop."

"I can't, Luke. It's too much." Already, the wave rushes in, preparing to carry me off somewhere into the deepest waters.

"You can. Look at you. Taking me like a fucking dream." He slides his hand between us, and his thrusts grow more erratic.

My clit is so sensitive, I feel like there's no way. Not again. Not so soon. It's impossible...

"God, you squeeze me so tight. That's it, beautiful, come for me. Steal every last drop out of me. It's all fucking yours." His teeth tug on my nipple, just as his thumb finds my clit, and I dissolve. This time, I go blank. The roaring sensation curls through me and sweeps me up in a darkened cloak, where I lose touch with my senses for a moment.

When I come back into my body, our mouths are desperate and hungry, locked in an intense fusion. The taste of myself on Luke as he slides our tongues together is so damn hot I can hardly breathe. He's buried deep inside me, unloading, pulsing.

Holding me so tight against him, it feels like we're both coming for an eternity.

"Jesus. Fuck." Panting against my mouth, Luke's groan is so primal it reaches into my chest and plants itself there.

It's the kind of noise that makes me never want to stop this with him. That tempts me to forget everything about who this man is to me, the complexities of how our lives are intertwined, and to throw caution to the wind.

How could anything else ever be this good?

"You make me crazy, you know that? This pussy..." He's so strong, lifting us easily and tumbling me onto my back.

With a hiss, he pulls out, but has a look on his face that tells me he's still not satisfied.

"Oh my god, Luke... No. I can't." My hands push at his head as he falls over me. Kissing and licking a trail down my body. There's no way in hell. I'm so out of my head with too much pleasure, too soon. A thundering torrent of emotion and over-stimulation pours through me, unrelenting, beating frantically through my veins.

"Lie still." He stares up at me with hooded, darkened eyes from just above my pussy.

I'm still trying to push him away. Trying to inch up the couch, close my legs, and escape whatever he's got planned for me next.

"No more. I can't take any more."

His palms are scalding hot against my knees. Pinning me in place.

"You were begging for my cock not long ago." He hovers over my pussy with his mouth, trapping me with those dark eyes, and spreads my legs wide for his inspection.

"This is too much," I whine, although even as I say the words, my fingers clench in his hair. Maybe I'm tugging him closer. Maybe I'm pushing him away. Maybe I'm just a total slut for this cowboy.

"Look at you. Leaking my cum." His gaze drifts down, and I can feel the slickness of him at my entrance. It's almost unbearable, having him so close, watching in rapt fascination at the evidence of both of us gathering there. Of the fact he's made a complete mess of me, and yet can't seem to get enough of being wedged between my thighs.

"Let me look after you." It's a quiet, gravelly murmur. Words that in such a voice, rumble right through me and drop deep into my chest. Latching onto something that had been floating around untethered for so long.

Luke doesn't wait for me to say anything in reply.

I can't.

It's too intimate. It feels like more than just sex when he looks at me like that with those words and traces of my pussy on his lips. I'm a fool if I'm reading more into it than the afterglow of orgasms.

However, he's not interested in waiting for my response. Luke takes care of me all the same; his mouth fastens over my entrance, and my back bows up off the couch, feeling the scrape of his beard and the insane pleasure he keeps giving me just when I truly think I can't take anymore.

He gathers up our cum and pushes it back inside me with two fingers, followed by wicked swirls of his tongue, pressing into me until I'm whining his name.

With every single second he treats me so perfectly, this man steals my heart and drives me out of my damn mind.

Before carrying me to bed and continuing to do just as he promised.

Taking care of me for the rest of the night.

CHAPTER 20

There are a dozen curious creatures in this part of the stables. All angling their long necks and letting out impatient snorts in order to get a glimpse at the girl out here helping with the chores this morning.

Skylar croons and chats away to each of them as she works her way through the stalls. She's taken over mucking out and shooed me off as soon as I showed her the ropes.

I've busied myself elsewhere... because I'm unable to keep off her. Every part of me wants to reach out and touch her in some way.

Not just sexually—I mean, that's undeniably part of my addiction to this girl—but in the way we seem to be able to spend time together so easily. It's effortless to be with her.

She's smart and quick to tease, and for someone like me who has enjoyed his own company for a very long fucking time, Skylar fits with that in a way I wasn't expecting.

We haven't even talked about Brad all that much, which I thought might be where things faltered between us. Once the fucking and tension was out of our system, I had worried that maybe we would have nothing to talk about beyond her being my son's best friend. That our worlds would be too distant from one another.

Instead, we've spent the past day and night together. *Talking*.

She showed me her store's Instagram, photos and videos of her floristry work—which is stunning—plans she's got for events and clients who have already booked her for the new year. Skylar's smile only grew brighter when she sheepishly told me about the dream she's had of growing different varieties of peonies, of having a farmgate style *pick your own* operation, while building a team to handle the shop front for her.

This girl has got budgets and spreadsheets and absolutely has her shit together. When I think back to being young and dumb and her age, I'm embarrassed to admit all I was doing was roping, riding, and chasing skirts.

Everything is done with such an eye for aesthetic detail, it's no surprise Skylar's busy as all hell.

In between phone calls with her parents and some other friends, she told me about her folks' travels and how they want her to fly to meet them somewhere during the summer.

I mean, admittedly, a lot of those conversations have been while naked or in between another round of hot-as-fuck sex, but there's a familiarity there between us.

In all honesty, I hadn't expected to find that sort of connection with anyone, let alone a girl half my age who I shouldn't even be looking at.

Something that was put into sharp perspective when Brad video called, and it made for a very awkward twenty minutes when both of us tried to pretend like we didn't spend all of Christmas with my tongue in her cunt.

"She's so glossy." Her voice glides in and interrupts my thoughts. I've been busy grooming my bay gelding, Fizz, lost in my own mind and didn't even hear her approaching.

"That she is. Fizzy loves a compliment, too." Sure enough she's nuzzling Skylar, looking for a bit of extra attention. "How's it going down there?"

"I think I'm all done. You might have to check my work, though, Mr. Rhodes."

Her lips roll together, and lashes flutter. Baby blues bounce between my eyes, down to my mouth, then up to my hat. She settles her gaze there, lingering, and her tongue darts out to wet her lips.

Tossing the brush into the bucket next to my boots, I tuck my hands in my jacket pockets and close the distance between us. Advancing slowly, watching eagerly as Skylar retreats with a sinful little smile playing on her lips, until her back makes contact with the wooden wall.

"Did you get distracted on the job, sweetheart?" I selfishly eat up the way her pupils dilate and lips part on a shallow exhale.

"Maybe." Small white puffs leave her lips with the heat of her breath on the crisp air.

It's way too goddamn cold out here to be sinking into her, even though that's a particular fantasy I've played out in my mind's eye one too many times over the past couple of days.

"Can I tell you a secret?"

"You can tell me anything." I lean one arm over her, high on the wall, brushing our bodies together.

She bites her bottom lip, and the glassy look in her eyes spells my impending doom. Because I know it, I know whatever comes out of this girl's mouth next, I'll agree to.

Her tiny fingers curl into the front of my jacket, and she goes up on tiptoes. I have to duck my head lower so that she can reach my ear and it sends a shudder roaming through me.

Illicit thoughts drift in of having days, months, years on end when this could be a reality between us.

"I'm sorry, Mr. Rhodes, but I forgot to put any panties on." Skylar's voice is a sultry whisper. "And I can feel you running down my thighs."

"Jesus." I swallow thickly. My pulse starts thudding hard as hoofbeats in my neck.

"Then you had to go and stroll around in that hat and those jeans... and..." She peeks up at me through a heavy curtain of lashes.

"Are you telling me that your needy little pussy is out here bare and slutty and dripping with my cum?" With my other hand not leaning on the wall, I rub my thumb back and forth across her bottom lip before tugging it down.

I'm fucking addicted to the way her pupils blow out when I treat her this way. A little bit stern, but mostly just teasing her and telling her how perfect she is.

Goddamn, if it doesn't make everything insanely hot that my cum is still inside her from when I had her bent over the bathroom counter this morning.

"Do you want to see?" Her words are soft. Delicate. Just like her.

Fuck. I might just forget my damn mind and propose to this girl.

"I didn't think I could find a way to fuck you out here, but I might have to change that plan." I press my thumb into her mouth, and the good girl she is, Skylar swirls her tongue around and laps at the pad.

Pushing off the wall, I grasp my hat and lift it off, placing it over her pastel pink waves.

As I sink down to my knees in front of her, those blue eyes widen, and her lips hang parted as she watches me.

I give her a wink as my fingers hook into her waistband.

"Suits you, sweetheart."

"Does it?" Her fingers seek out my hair in the way I'm absolutely addicted to. I want those nails digging into my scalp and tugging hard as often as possible.

"*Mmmm*. You're gonna have to let me see you wear it from another angle, just so I can really get a good look at you." I flick the button on her jeans. "I think you're gonna have to ride me with *only* that on. Right now, there are too many clothes on this perfect body for me to be certain."

She laughs, a light tinkling feminine sound, the kind of playful noise that is so foreign in this barn, but one that feels so fucking right. Her stomach caves as my fingers press against the softness of her skin.

Just as I work her jeans down, just as I lean forward to lick a long line over her pouty clit—plump and begging for my attention—and suck it into my mouth, there's the sound of a vehicle outside.

Tires crunch over the snow, muffled music plays as the two people I certainly have no interest in seeing pull up next to the barn.

"Oh my god." The fingers that should be guiding me to exactly where Skylar wants my long, slow kisses are now tugging me off her. "Is it Brad?"

I hastily wipe my mouth on the back of my hand. Fucking fuck.

"Christ. Do you want me to get rid of him?" I get to my feet, helping pull her jeans back up. I'd gladly give anything, find any excuse under the sun, to tell my son to fuck right off right now.

She bats my hands away. Eyes gone round as the moon.

"Just go stall him," she hisses.

I hate everything about what this means... that our time has ended in an abrupt halt. If I'd known this morning was our last chance to be alone together, I wouldn't have come to the stables at all.

"It's ok. Go." She jerks her head and fastens her jeans, then turns. Only, she falters for a second and quickly pulls my hat off and thrusts it back into my hands before she vanishes out of the stall.

Slipping away from me without an opportunity for a proper goodbye.

CHAPTER 21

"You can't leave town. Stay." Brad crosses his arms. "What the fuck are you gonna do, Sky? Have the world's most miserable New Year pity party all by yourself?"

I'm being stared down by my best friend and his boyfriend, who are determined to keep me here stuck in torturous longing for the man sleeping in the room across the hall.

Because even though Brad and Flinn have their own home on this ranch, they've been my own personal shadows since arriving back.

Under normal circumstances, this is exactly how things would be between us if I ever came to stay. We'd be in each other's back pockets from dawn until long after midnight.

Except now, I'm painfully aware of the other Rhodes man in this house, who I haven't seen since our near miss at the stables yesterday morning.

"Look, it's only three more sleeps until New Year's Eve."

"And you know he's going to be fucking insufferable if you don't stay, so do me a solid, would you, please, love?" Flinn looks up from his phone where we're all sitting around the farmhouse kitchen table.

The one I was splayed out on, covered in whiskey and Lucas Rhode's wicked mouth only a few nights ago.

"Fine. Fine. I'll stay for your silly little party." I tease. "But in return, you gotta help me get my tire and stealth-rescue my car."

"You sure you don't want to just claim it got stolen? We could torch it and dump it out on a back road somewhere?"

"Oh my god. Are you insane? I don't need Sheriff Hayes on my ass, thank you."

Brad chuckles. "He's hot. I wouldn't mind that man being all up in my business."

From across the other side of the table, Flinn gives him an eye roll. "I'm literally *right here*."

"Oh, don't pretend like you haven't checked that man's ass out in a pair of jeans before."

"Either way," I interrupt the man-crush going on over our local Sheriff. "We're not disposing of my car. Don't be ridiculous, Bradford Rhodes."

"What? It's an ugly fucking ride." He shrugs, gets up and starts rummaging in the fridge.

"It's served me well, I'll have you know." I huff.

"Ok, so let's make a plan to get your tire sorted and grab your car." Flinn ignores his idiotic boyfriend and taps on his phone screen. "The garage is open today but closes again until after the new year. So today's our chance to get this shit done."

"Thank you, Flinny. At least one of you assholes is helpful."

"Hey, Dad... you need anything from town? We're going in to sort out Sky's car." Brad calls out, and that's when I feel his presence.

My cheeks immediately heat, and I have to fight every urge in my blood to turn around in my chair. I want to throw myself into his arms so goddamn badly it hurts. Which is why I can't let myself even glance his way, because if I do, it'll be too obvious. There isn't a chance in hell I could keep my head on straight or emotions in check when it comes to that man.

The familiar deep, rich sound of him clearing his throat sends goosebumps flying over my skin. "I'll text you a list."

"Sweet. Anything you want us to pick you up for dinner?" Brad heads over to collect our jackets, and yet I keep myself rooted firmly in place. Pretending to read something on my phone.

"No, I'm good. You kids do your own thing for dinner." That's all he says, and then as quickly as he appeared, he's gone.

I hear Brad and Flinn chatting animatedly as I trail after them out of the house, and we all pile into their truck, but I'm only half paying attention to anything in my surroundings. My mind is stuck in a loop of memories of Luke's touch, his kisses, his lips tipping up into a small smile.

The guys occupy the front seats, and as I buckle myself in, my phone vibrates in my pocket.

BRAD'S DAD:

> I wish I could be the one to help you today.

> I hate that I can't.

My eyes shoot up to my friend, who is driving and playing *rock, paper, scissors* with his boyfriend to decide what to have for dinner.

Oh my god. I have to bite the inside of my cheek because I might just swoon right out of this vehicle.

> I wish you could, too.

God, there are so many other things I want to say to him. *I miss you already. I want to feel your arms around me. I think I'm in love with you.*

Except it's not possible. Nothing between us was ever going to be more than a temporary bit of fun. To work through the sexual chemistry we have, but both knew it was going to end as soon as Brad came home.

> Probably for the best.

Really?

> With how beautiful you look today…
>
> Let's just say that tire might have been the last thing on my mind.

I'm blushing so damn hard right now. I have to sink into my coat collar to avoid giving away the goofy look on my face.

Mr. Rhodes.

Are you flirting with me?

> I shouldn't be.

Do you want to?

Butterflies erupt in my stomach, watching the tiny dots bounce on the screen for what seems like an eternity, stopping and starting before his reply finally comes through.

> Sweetheart, I want everything when it comes to you.

CHAPTER 22

My son is officially the biggest cock block I've ever met.

After spending the day yesterday helping Skylar get a new tire, and to replace her spare, *and* make sure she was fixed up and able to drive safely to park up here at the ranch, I suppose I should be proud of him.

When in reality, I'm insanely fucking jealous of the fact he and Flinn have been able to take care of her in all the ways I want to be able to.

It's been two nights.

Two nights without her, when she's been in the guest room just across the hall, I've laid in bed restlessly arguing with myself and my moral fiber. Weighing up the possibility of whether I can steal her away to be with me in the midnight hours when no one could possibly know, except for our guilty consciences.

Because Skylar made it clear she wouldn't do anything to hurt Brad, and that she doesn't want this to ruin my relationship with him.

So, who am I to go against her wishes?

The easiest solution has been to stay away. To find a hundred and one jobs to do around the ranch and let them all hang out together, getting things ready for this New Year's Eve party. This is how everything would *usually* be in the past when Skylar spent time here.

Except, in all those years, all that time she spent around the place, that wasn't when she was on my mind twenty-four-fucking-seven. Now she is, and I can't erase her from my thoughts.

The three of them have been hanging out here at the house since Brad and Flinn's place is barely more than a single-room cabin. It works perfectly for just the two of them, but isn't exactly big enough for having guests over. Right now, the guys are sprawled out side by side on the couch, with some shitty action movie pulled up on the big screen. All I can see is the backs of their heads, while Skylar is curled up in one of the large armchairs over by the window, giving me a perfect view of her side profile. Her Kindle is balanced on her lap, and I'm immediately transported back to Christmas Day, lying with her tucked against my side on the couch... and everything that came after.

Fuck.

I have to subtly readjust myself as I linger in the kitchen. Truth be told, I walked in, saw Skylar, and promptly forgot what I meant to come in here for.

She's so much better at this than me, managing to keep a straight face and not look my way every three seconds, which is all I seem to be able to do whenever we're in the same room.

Thank fuck, because if it were up to me, I would have given our entire secret away far too quickly.

After texting her briefly when they went to get her tire replaced and collect her car, I've opened and composed what feels like a hundred new messages. Only, each time I inevitably hit delete, seeing as I shouldn't be saying any of the shit I actually want to say.

There's also always too much of a risk my son will pick up her phone, or see what's on the screen, which has been enough to have me silently cursing and shoving my phone back in my pocket.

However, right now, I can see that the guys are occupied with whatever they're watching. Brad might even be asleep from what I can tell.

> Stop biting your lip so hard.

Crossing my ankles, I lean my ass back against the sink. Partly hidden by the large island in the middle of the kitchen, it's easy to hang back here while still being able to see through the open-plan layout to the lounge.

I don't hear her phone make a sound, however, as I watch on, she picks it up immediately, which leads my pulse to race a little harder.

Has she been keeping it on silent, just in case I do text her again?

Ever the tease, Skylar quickly types on the screen, without looking my way or allowing her expression to change. If anyone were to look at her, she could be texting her goddamn grandmother for all they would know.

My phone buzzes in my palm.

SWEETHEART:

> Sorry, but it's not easy.

> Not when you're making it impossible for a girl to concentrate.

> Do I distract you?

> No.

> I can see you squirming.

You don't 'distract' me.

Because it's impossible to be a distraction when I already can't stop thinking about you.

> Good.

> Then I'm not the only one going insane over here.

I heard you get up during the night.

Kinda hoped it was because you were gonna sneak into my room...

Even though I know we can't.

> Sweetheart, it took everything in me not to.

> I honestly don't know if I can fight it anymore.

We said we wouldn't.

> I know.

> But, I'm a terrible fucking person.

> I can't stay away from you.

I see her shift around in her seat, and if I didn't know any better I'd say she looks incredibly turned on.

"I'm gonna go take a shower." Skylar hops up out of her chair. The other two barely even move, just make a grunting sort of noise in acknowledgement that is more reminiscent of Brad as a teenager rather than a young man in his twenties. "You guys keep watching, and I'll reheat some leftovers for us for dinner once I'm done, yeah?"

She scoops her phone and Kindle up, then crosses toward the stairs.

Our eyes lock.

Those baby blues are almost turned to a deep shade of sapphire, pupils blown out with lust.

My cock is already straining against the front of my jeans.

I let her carry on up to the guest room, hanging impatiently in the kitchen, listening to each footstep, trying to figure out how goddamn long I need to wait before following straight after her. Brad and Flinn seem oblivious to the fact I'm even here, engrossed in what they're watching, or possibly both half asleep anyway.

The sound of water running drifts down from upstairs.

I'm going to hell for even contemplating this.

It takes everything in me not to mount the steps two at a time. Creeping up as quietly as possible.

Skylar has left her bedroom door open just a crack, and I slip inside, twisting and lifting the handle in exactly the way I know will allow it to shut on silent hinges.

A trail of clothes leads me straight to the bathroom, and when I step through the doorway, my girl is already naked and wet. Her spine rests against the tiled walk-in shower, with swirling steam filling the room, and a glide of soapy bubbles coats those perfect fucking tits and softness of her stomach.

She hits me with eyes I could goddamn drown in, and lifts a finger to her lips.

My eyes drop down to see where her other hand dips in between her thighs. Already working herself, rubbing in small circles over her clit.

I don't need a second fucking invitation.

My clothes hit the floor, and I'm on her, barely stifling a groan as I hoist her legs around my waist. Holding her tight, with fingers clung around my neck, I shove inside that velvety channel I've been fantasizing about. Having to settle instead for fucking my fist the past couple of nights, choking on her name, desperately missing being wrapped together just like this.

"Oh god." She lets out a soft moan as my cock shoves deep inside. I almost bite my tongue in half with how unbelievably slick she is. This girl is an absolute mess, her pussy is drenched, and it makes me goddamn feral to know this is the state she's in while thinking about me.

Using one arm to band her soft body against mine, I cover her mouth with my free hand.

"Shh, sweetheart. You're going to get us caught making slutty little noises like that," I whisper. The water beats down on my back, and I'm sure no one could hear a thing even if they were standing right outside the door, but we both know it's the middle of the afternoon, and we've not got much time.

Her eyes flash, and she laps her tongue against my palm. The curve of her lips forming a smile beneath my touch is everything.

I drive my hips forward.

Skylar's nails dig into my nape, and she tightens around me like a fucking dream.

It's fast and desperate between us; my hips pump into her, keeping her body pressed up against the wall, and I lose any sense of time.

I know it has to be quick. I know I can't linger here. I know we're already crossing that line we said we wouldn't once the snow cleared.

But holy fuck, this girl is everything.

She keeps squeezing me tighter and tighter, and it's obvious she's as wound up in a frenzy as I am. The headiness of this moment is almost too much. My teeth are gritted against the sounds that want to burst out of me, that want to explode in a series of grunts and guttural roars of pleasure in time with my dick. Tingling builds in my balls and at the base of my spine as I feel my climax racing forward.

Skylar's fingers pull on my hair harder and harder as I feel her body tense up. I drive in deep, thrusting, snapping my hips, chasing the sensation of release we've both been in agony without, because I know it's been the same for her.

I quickly withdraw my hand and replace that point of contact with my mouth. Covering hers with my own in a harsh, desperate kiss. Seeking out her clit, everything is in a race to the finish line, when all I want to do is sink into her over and over. I wish we had hours ahead to indulge in as many orgasms as possible, but this right here, a quick fuck in her shower, is what I'll take if that's all I can have of her.

She gasps against my lips, trying her hardest to stay quiet, and I suck down on her tongue as I rub hard over her swollen, slippery clit.

My gorgeous girl, my ultimate temptation, absolutely shatters like a dream. She can't help the noise she makes into my mouth, and I do my best to swallow it down. As she squeezes the life out of me, like a fist wrapped around my length, my own wave peaks and crashes. My cock throbs as I plunge forward and hold, jerking and pulsing inside her. Cum shoots deep, and it all feels so good; it's always so good with her, feeling like it goes on and on. Like I can't stop coming.

She's still fluttering and rippling around my length. Our mouths are nothing but sloppy kisses as our hearts both thunder in time to the water pounding down.

I just want to keep holding her.

I want to march her to that bed and lick her cunt, to taste both of us there, to hear her moan my name over and over as her thighs clamp down around my head.

Only, we can't fucking do any of those things.

She has to go downstairs, and I have to make myself scarce once more.

CHAPTER 23

Skylar

"You need me to do what, with the what?" I blink at Brad. He should know by now I'm not to be trusted with anything important in this kitchen. *Any* kitchen.

"You'll be fine, Sky. Just keep an eye on the pan, and if anything starts to stick, just turn it." He shrugs into his coat, keys jangling. "I gotta go pick up a few more things from the grocery store for the party tomorrow; I'll be half an hour, tops."

"Don't come for me if these meatballs are all burnt to fuck by the time you get back." I cross my arms and give him a petulant eye roll.

"I have faith in you." He calls over his shoulder.

"No, you don't," I shout after him. "At least bring me back some ice cream, bitch."

The sound of the front door shutting is all I get in reply. I'm tugging out my phone from my back pocket to text him my demands for rich, chocolatey, frozen goodness, when I feel the heat of a broad chest behind me. The proximity and suddenness of where he's just appeared from makes the fine hairs stand up on my arms.

"Are these supposed to be charred?" Luke's voice is so close it makes me jump.

"What? No..." I spin round in an immediate panic, shoving at his immovable shoulder to get a proper look at the pan. They were fine and sizzling and definitely *not* burnt two minutes ago. "All I did was check my phone; they can't be burnt already."

That's when I realize what's really going on. The mountain of a man beside me has his hand over his mouth, dark eyes twinkling with mirth.

Lucas Rhodes is laughing at me.

"Oh. Not funny. Not funny at all." I pout.

"You're cute. Grab yourself a drink, and I'll keep an eye on all this." Luke nudges my hip with his thigh and I suck in a sharp breath. My eyes immediately fly up to check our surroundings, but the house is quiet. We're the only ones here.

"Flinn's down at their place. I just saw him as I left the stables, and Brad won't be back for a little bit longer." He absently tucks a strand of hair behind my ear, and I just about dissolve into a puddle on the floor, right there, in the middle of the kitchen.

"Do you want something?" My voice is suddenly hoarse. Me? My entire heart and soul, perhaps?

"A beer would be perfect." He sets about fussing with the tongs and the pan, and I think my heart is suddenly about three times too big for my chest.

I grab each of us a drink and hand him over one. As I do so, he hooks my pinky finger with his, not letting me step away.

"I was serious yesterday." That rich, gritty voice rumbles through my senses. "I can't stay away from you, sweetheart... but you say the word, and I'll respect that. I'll keep my distance, alright?"

"I just wish..." I swallow thickly. Not entirely sure what I want to say in this moment.

"Your friendship is more important, I get that. Brad means the world to both of us. I couldn't live with myself if my selfishness ruined any aspect of what you have as friends."

A heavy sigh gusts out of my lungs. I have to fight the urge to sink against his chest and wrap my arms around his broad torso.

Luke holds my chin, sweeping his thumb over my bottom lip. "In another life. In *any* other life, I'd track you down and wouldn't let you go. You're worth that and so much more, Skylar."

I'm gaping up at him. Frozen in place at the sincerity in his words and tenderness in his usually chiseled, gruff exterior.

Goddamn this man for stealing my heart when I know that I can't stay here beyond tomorrow.

Words aren't forming, even though I'm trying, and failing, to find the right thing to say in reply. To articulate the increasingly complicated set of feelings I have for this cowboy.

But the outside world beats me to it. The front door bangs, and I hear Flinn come inside, midway through a conversation on the phone as he does so. His boots thud one by one as he kicks them off in the hallway, and that's my cue to put some distance between us.

Luke sets his beer down and turns back to the pan on the stove, but not before sliding me one last look that will stay imprinted on my mind forever.

"Remember all that when the next guy comes along."

CHAPTER 24

Lucas

My house is filled with people, music, and laughter.

Brad is in his fucking element, practically buzzing with joy as he makes sure everyone is enjoying themselves and putting on one heck of a night to celebrate the ranch.

I gotta hand it to him, the kid knows the value of networking and being *peopley*. Thank fuck he's got the gift because I certainly don't.

Instead, I've been firmly planted in front of the grill, keeping busy with the night air for company and an excuse to be away from the crowd. There are plenty of people I know here tonight, and most have sought me out for a chance to chat and catch up, shooting the shit before heading back inside into the warm.

Another reason I've kept myself occupied in this spot, is to not follow Skylar around like some kind of stray dog. The girl deserves a night with her friends, and I wish it was a different set of circumstances between us, but it's easier this way.

The night is crisp, not below freezing, but cold enough that I've been pleased to have a hot flame to warm myself in front of.

It's getting closer to midnight, and I know I should probably put in an appearance inside. Mingle, or some shit.

Just as I'm steeling myself to enter the house, my phone buzzes in my pocket. That small vibration sends a twitch through my lips and a jerk straight to my cock.

SWEETHEART:

> Where are you?

>> Outside, packing up the grill.

>> Having fun?

> Not as much as if you were here.

> I know you've been hiding.

I catch myself smirking at my phone like a goddamn teenager.

>> How much have you had to drink?

> Not much, a couple earlier on.

>> Aren't you enjoying yourself?

> I've been waiting for midnight...

>> What happens at midnight?

> You meet me at the barn.

A dark groan escapes out of me as I scrub one hand over my mouth at the sight of those six words on screen.

>> I don't think that's possible.

> There are too many people. How are you gonna slip away?

> I've already told Brad my parents want to video call me at twelve, so I'll need to disappear off somewhere quiet to chat with them.

> Don't you think it's too risky?

> Well, either you meet me there and fuck me at midnight, or you can watch me ride my fingers until I make myself come when I send you the video.
>
> Your choice.

Holy crap. This girl. She knows I've already lost this battle, I don't even need to see her face to know the way her lips will be quirking, the way her blue eyes will be sparkling.

> You've got two minutes to get your ass out of that party.
>
> The only way you're gonna be falling apart is if my cock is filling your perfect cunt.

> Yes, Daddy.

> Jesus.
>
> You're trying to kill me.

> Well, I'm wet and need you inside me.

> Clock's ticking. One minute.

This time, instead of text in reply, an image comes through. It's of her hand holding a bottle of whiskey, and even though the background is dark, I can see that she's already two steps ahead of me.

Skylar is already inside the barn.

My pulse hammers in my neck as I slide the wooden door closed behind me.

It's dark in here, and the horses make little huffing noises, asking me what the fuck is going on and why we're intruding on them at this time of night.

There's a faint glow from the far end, inside the tack room, and I head straight there.

Sure enough, that's where I find my girl.

Except, I stop in my tracks in the doorway when I see her. She's wrapped up in her coat, but her makeup is bolder than usual, her hair styled into loose curls. She's got the same boots and tights on as the first night she hurtled back into my life when I picked her up amongst the snow.

Stunning doesn't even do Skylar Addams justice.

She's perched on a saddle stand and wiggles the neck of the bottle in my direction, eyes bouncing over me.

"You look hot as fuck." She beams my way, and I don't know what the hell I've done to deserve a single moment with this girl.

My tongue pokes against the side of my mouth, and I allow the weight of my gaze to linger on every inch of her in return.

"It's a good thing I didn't see you earlier, or we might not have made it to midnight without me trying to steal you away."

Skylar blushes and it's cute as hell.

"You want to have a drink with me?"

"No." My boots thud as I cross the space between us.

The sweetest little laugh erupts from her as she lets me steal the whiskey and set it on the shelf before cupping her face, tasting those lips, sinking our mouths together in a deep fucking kiss. One that I've been dreaming of in a constant loop of memories since our desperately quick moment in the shower.

"How long do we have?" Drawing back, I already know it won't ever be goddamn long enough.

Skylar makes a seductive little noise against my lips. "How fast can you get inside me?"

Reaching up, I grab my hat, and set it over her hair, brushing a few loose strands behind her ear as I do so.

"You see, that's where we've got a problem, sweetheart." My palms find her thighs, and I lower myself onto my knees in between her parted legs. The place I will happily always occupy for this girl. "I don't want to do anything *fast*. I want to take my time, and I want to spend hours lost inside this perfect cunt of yours."

She lets out a little moan as I hitch her coat higher and hook the soft jersey material of her dress at the same time. My good girl braces herself so I can separate her thighs even wider.

"Then, give me your phone." Skylar runs her fingers through my hair, tugging a little to tilt my head up toward her.

My heart stalls.

"Are you serious?"

"I want to watch. You want to take your time. Sounds like a good compromise if you can spend as much time replaying this moment as you want." Her teeth catch that pouty bottom lip, and I damn near groan.

"How the fuck are you so perfect?" I dig my phone out of my pocket, unlock the screen, and hand it to her.

"Better save this somewhere safe." Skylar's voice is a little husky as she hits me with the most tempting of looks, pink hair framing her gorgeous heart-shaped face, my hat perched on top of her head. It's a sight I'm already imprinting and committing to memory, with or without a video on my phone.

Her fingers sink into my hair once again with a soft hum of pleasure, and that's when I realize she's already recording. The light of the camera flash plays over the place where my palms wrap her thighs, and she pans up to where she holds onto my hair, threading her grip in the spot where I know my streak of white stands out.

"Are you gonna keep quiet for me? Or do you want to be loud? Do you want all your sweet little moans recorded on camera?"

I don't give her time to answer, maybe because part of me isn't sure it's a good idea to have her saying anything. Just in case someone ever did watch this when they shouldn't, I selfishly don't want anyone to know it's her.

Working the coat and dress all the way up to sit above her hips, that's when I have to pause. Skylar holds on to my head a little tighter, keeping the camera trained on my face, and I run my tongue across the swell of her inner thigh, giving her a stern glare as I do so.

"We've talked about this, sweetheart." My teeth nip her delicate flesh, and she yanks harder on my hair in response. "It looks like you've forgotten your panties... again."

A soft little noise gusts past her lips, like she's as relieved as I am we've somehow found a way to be in this position once more.

This time, my girl is completely bare.

Garters hold her tights up, hooked to a belt around her waist, and holy fuck I swear my heart nearly stops at how sexy this girl is. Her hips shift as my mouth roams closer and closer.

The whole time, I'm keeping my eyes fixed on her. Looking straight into that camera lens because I don't know if she'll ever keep a copy of this video for herself, but goddamn, do I want her to know exactly how obsessed I am with every little thing.

"Look at your pretty little cunt. Already dripping wet, and I haven't even touched you yet."

Above me, she angles the camera so that her pussy and my mouth is the main show. My hands come up to push her thighs wide, and using each thumb, I part her. It's lewd and filthy, and she's entirely goddamn gorgeous. Swollen and slick, ready to be devoured.

"You know what would happen if I had you to myself all night? I'd lick this pretty little cunt until you begged me to stop. I'd have you shaking and soaking my face and telling me you couldn't take any more, but we'd both know that's a lie. Because you want this all day and all night long, don't you, sweetheart?"

I'm not interested in waiting for a reply; my mouth fastens down over her clit, and Skylar bucks as my tongue slides over her. She makes the most gorgeous noises above me, keeping the camera fixed on where I'm lapping and sucking and working her hard. We don't have the luxury of time, and I need at least a couple of orgasms out of her.

If this is the last moment, truly the *last*, then I need to taste her falling apart on my tongue.

Which doesn't take long.

Skylar is a goddamn dream, shaking and whimpering as I feel her get close to the edge. Sucking down on her clit, my girl dissolves. Her fingers pull on my hair so hard it stings, but I couldn't care less.

Pushing to my feet, my cock is a steel bar, ready to shove into the tight, velvety heat of her.

"This is how perfect you are. The reason I could get lost

between your thighs all fucking night long." With one hand, I wrap hers and guide the camera up to make sure she captures this moment. Kissing her, sliding our tongues together, and letting her taste herself there.

Skylar moans into my mouth, her fingers clutch the front of my jacket to steady herself.

In the distance, there's a whole lot of noise that floats on the night air from up at the house.

A countdown.

"Goddamn, I need you wrapped around me, right fucking now." Nipping her bottom lip, I angle her hand to make sure she films what comes next.

Freeing my straining cock, I fist myself and give a few long strokes and eat up the way her eyes follow the glide of my fist.

"Happy New Year, sweetheart," I murmur, positioning myself at her entrance and sliding forward to fit the tip just inside. She's already dripping and messy and takes me perfectly. Stretching and welcoming me into that soft, satiny channel.

The sight of us joined like this is so hot, my balls are already tightening up. Pressure and anticipation are already winding together at the base of my spine.

"I'll never fucking get over this. I'll never fucking get over you." My hips steadily work forward until I'm all the way to the hilt, and her pussy ripples around me.

Holy fuck.

Skylar whimpers louder, biting her lip as hard as she can to keep quiet, her eyes still fixed on the carnal image of where our bodies are joined. She holds the camera trained on that part of us as I withdraw right to the tip. Coated in the sheen of her arousal and glistening in the light of the camera.

"Christ. That's so fucking sexy." My voice is a deep rasp.

BOUQUETS & BUCKLES

I slide forward, nearly losing it completely when she clamps down around me. She's fighting it, already lingering close to the edge. Maybe it's the fact we're filming this moment. Maybe it's the fact we both know this is really it—the last time we can do this. Maybe it's the fact we've only got minutes left before I have to somehow get her back to the house without looking like she's just had her brains fucked out.

Whatever it is, it drags us both to the edge, real fucking fast this time around.

I pump in and out, hooking one of her legs high so I can really open her up to show the camera exactly how insanely good this moment is.

That's when I feel her squeeze harder, tightening around me, muffled desperate noises coming out in time with each punch of my hips. Skylar's just as close to falling apart as I am. Using my thumb, I find her clit and add that pressure I know will get her there.

I don't even know what I'm saying. It's a string of filthy fucking words. Telling her how perfect her cunt is. That she's gorgeous when she's leaking my cum. How I'd spend all night owning every single one of her pretty little holes if I could. That she's my perfect little slut, who deserves to be bent over right here next to the saddles while I pump her full.

Skylar detonates on a low moan. Clamping down and gasping. It's all so fucking intense that my own release follows right behind. My balls draw up, my dick jerks, and I bury myself to the hilt. Holding there as my seed spills and coats her channel, hardly able to register anything except for the pounding rush of blood in my ears.

Both her arms wrap around the back of my neck, filming long forgotten, as Skylar seeks out my mouth. I cradle the back of her head, holding my hat so it gives me access to her mouth but doesn't tumble to the dirt. We kiss in a way that reminds me of being so much younger, without the burdens of being a solo parent, without the stresses and pressures that come with running this ranch. Being with her eases so much of that, in a way I can't fucking explain. As she hums and melts against my mouth, lapping at my tongue and kissing me with all the warmth and goodness that is just *her*, I know it just feels right holding her. As if all those things that on the bleakest day feel like such a struggle, I'd easily face them knowing Skylar Addams was mine.

God, I want to tell her, but that would be madness.

She's leaving first thing in the morning, and her life is waiting for her. I'd never ask her to give up that dream she's working on, and I'd never risk her friendship with my son.

This is the type of kiss that lets me tell Skylar I'm in love with her, but it's also the one that tells this beautiful girl that I'm letting her go.

Even though I hate that I have to.

I hate that we'll still be circling each other in that inevitable way people do when there's a connecting point between us— Brad. It kills me to think I'm going to be stuck on the sidelines, seeing her continue to live out her life and thrive.

As we pull back and I study her in the deep shadows, Skylar looks at me with that same expression as a year ago when she sat in the front seat of my truck with her hand resting on the door.

Only this time, she brings my phone back around and angles it so that it takes in the sight of her wearing my hat.

A sight I'm never going to be able to stop replaying in my mind's eye.

I'm still buried deep inside her when she brings our mouths back to touching. Our lips brush together with the warmth and wetness there of our kisses.

This time she positions the camera to record the way we're joined, and she brushes her mouth over mine, nudging our noses together. Skylar's voice is a gentle, feather-like sound playing over my mouth.

"Thank you for taking care of me... Happy New Year, Mr. Rhodes."

CHAPTER 25
One Month Later
Skylar

"You can drop by anytime after ten a.m. tomorrow and collect the arrangement, Ms. Heartford."

I feel the vibration in my palm, letting me know I have another call incoming. Pulling the phone away from my ear a little, I see *Brad* flash up on the screen.

That second of recognition is immediately followed by the pout in my heart that it's not the name I want to see on my phone. I love my best friend with my whole chest, but fuck if I don't have a whole lot of emotional baggage ready to tumble out of the closet after what happened between me and Luke.

His father.

The cowboy I fell in love with. Agonizingly so.

"Perfect, see you then." I drag my brain back to the job at hand before wrapping up the call. Taking a big, grounding breath, I hit the missed call notification, redialing the younger of the two Rhodes men.

Brad picks up immediately.

"What are you up to tonight?" He sounds like he's got a mouthful of food.

"I've got a hot date." I pin my phone against my ear with my shoulder and use both hands to start fussing with the gorgeous bouquet being picked up any minute now. A guy called in earlier to order these flowers, all sweaty palms and nerves, because he's proposing to his girlfriend tonight. It was very sweet, and he asked me what I thought about every detail he's got planned for the special moment. Based on how much thought and planning he's put into this, I told him she'll be swept off her feet.

"A date? You do?" Brad sounds stunned.

"Don't be so shocked down to your cute lil' bisexual booties."

"Are you fucking with me?"

That makes me frown. "Since when did I have to report my every single move to you, hmm?"

"Sky..." He scolds.

"What? I do. It's this very sexy evening I've got going on. It's called being a small business owner who has to be responsible and do her taxes." I tug on a length of ribbon from the holder, snipping it off, and begin to tie a bow around the gathered stems.

"So, not an actual date?"

"It's as close as I'll get, B." I laugh at how dismally boring my life is. Not bitter about it, at all. "Super romantic, though. Between my laptop... my spreadsheet... a bit of wine, throw in some cheese, put on a facemask, it's a whole thing."

"Well, let me come crash your incredibly lame night, and I can try help, or at the very least I'll do facemasks with you and feed you ice cream."

"Salted Caramel?"

"I've got a pint of that and chocolate fudge. Didn't know what your broken heart would be in the mood for."

I pause. Licking my lips as I try to figure out how to respond.

"You know I'm long over Jeremy. You don't have to mother-hen me. I'm honestly fine." Sweeping my palm across the workbench, I gather up the scattered off-cuts of stems from the arrangement and toss them in the trash.

After the scene I discovered on Christmas Eve, I cut all contact and blocked his ass everywhere. He can enjoy whoever his kitchen blow-job-blondey is. I'll gladly never see the prick ever again.

"I'm not talking about wank face Jeremy."

My stomach drops.

"I'm talking about whatever jerk you hooked up with on New Year's and have been moping around about ever since."

"I didn't—"

"Look. I'm gonna be on your front porch at six. So you can try to wriggle out of telling me everything then, but spoiler alert, I'm gonna get it out of you."

The door to my shop opens, with the nervous fiancé-to-be arriving right on time to collect his flowers.

"I gotta go, B."

"Facemasks and spilling your guts start at six."

"You suck," I hiss.

"I do. Very well, might I add. Just ask Flinn how good my *sucking* is."

I hang up on his hysterical laughter and flash a bright smile while holding out the perfect bouquet to symbolize *love*.

Meanwhile, my heart aches for the loss of my own.

CHAPTER 26

Skylar

There's a half-eaten wedge of brie, two slices of leftover pizza, and a bottle of white wine occupying my otherwise empty fridge.

At least that's dinner sorted for this evening.

Brad knows me well enough that he'll either eat before he comes over or turn up with takeout of some kind.

I've been a fluttering bundle of nerves since his phone call earlier, trying to figure out the best way to sidestep this entire conversation.

There were a few single guys at the New Year party, but Brad is friendly with all of them back in Crimson Ridge, so I can't pretend to shrug it off as if it was some stranger he doesn't know.

I grab everything out of the fridge, which now glares back at me woefully bare, and toss the pizza in the microwave.

The clock tells me I've got five minutes until he's going to arrive, so I go in search of my clay face mask in the bathroom.

Hell, my reflection isn't exactly a sight that will give Brad any confidence that I'm not out here being heartbroken. My hair is gathered up in two messy buns, my oversized hoodie drowns me, and I've got comfy sweats tucked into my even comfier socks.

But, fuck it, I've got my body weight in cheese and chocolate ice cream to consume. Who cares if I'm sporting trash panda chic? Certainly not the girl who has to figure out a way not to blurt out to her friend that she'd rather be worshiping his dad's cock.

I scoop out a little of the face mask and smear two fingers across my cheek in charcoal gray. Just as I'm about to start layering that bitch on thick, my doorbell rings.

God. Here we fucking go.

With an exaggerated sigh through my nose, I patter my way to the front door, drooping the tub of facemask I'd been carrying on the kitchen counter as I go past.

"Hope you brought food, 'cause I will cut a bitch if you try to steal my piz—"

My throat closes over mid-sentence.

Dark eyes find mine from beneath the brim of a hat I've been dreaming about for weeks on end. A broad chest fills my vision. The scent of leather and the faint hint of soap engulfs me.

"Hey."

I blink like a barn owl. Lucas Rhodes is on my doorstep.

"I did bring you something to eat, hopefully that's ok?"

Oh my god. My knees feel like they're going to buckle.

"Luke? What are you doing here?"

"Can I come in?" His lips twitch a little as his eyes sweep over me, leaving a trail of goosebumps in their wake.

"Are you carrying a crock pot?"

"It's called a casserole dish, actually. Do you have mud on your face?" He counters.

I want to die right here. I *do* have mud on my face, and I've got sweats on, and I'm wearing my baggiest, comfiest, least sexy outfit I could possibly have chosen.

Meanwhile, this man looks like the angels plucked him straight from cowboy heaven and delivered him to my door.

"Why are you here?" My knuckles turn white around the door handle.

Luke's brows crease, and he hesitates a moment, sending my pulse into an erratic, thudding mess.

"I told Brad everything. Well, more accurately, he harassed me nonstop after you left, kept on at me until he wore me down, and I told him what was wrong with me."

Oh god. My face pales.

Luke's expression isn't giving me any clues. Is Brad upset? Angry? When I spoke to him earlier, he seemed fine...

"He was a bit weirded out at first, but to be honest, Skylar, it's been him convincing me for the past few weeks that I needed to come here and see you."

"Weeks? Brad has known for weeks?" I whisper screech. Eyes nearly hanging out of my head.

"My kid is a lot of things, but I didn't expect him to be so... uhh... enthusiastic about me coming over here."

"Luke... I..."

My heart is doing backflips and somersaults, but I'm so uncertain what this actually means. We haven't spoken since that final night we had together on New Year. No matter how many times I went to text him, I couldn't bring myself to press send because I didn't want to give hope a chance to bloom.

"Skylar, I had to come and see you. I've been battling with myself this past month because all I want is for you to be happy. You've got your life, your business, so much ahead of you, and it would eat away at me if I fucked any of that up by selfishly knocking on your door.

"But you gotta know, I was serious when I said *in another*

life... and maybe, just maybe, this is our life after all. If there's any chance you might want to let me be part of yours, I gotta have you know my heart is here. It's with you, even if this isn't something you want. I fell harder than I knew could be possible in just a few short days, and I miss you. So fucking much."

I'm not sure I remember how to breathe. It's like I can't process what he's saying because up until five minutes ago, all of this, everything he's laid out that I'd so desperately longed for didn't seem possible.

My silence causes his shoulders to drop a little.

"I sprung this on you... I'm sorry, it was Brad's idea to do some big romantic gesture, but I can go." His voice drops into a soft sigh. "At least let me put this inside for you." Luke gestures at me with the lidded ceramic dish he's still holding in his big hands.

"Just set it down there." I point at the floor.

Luke's jaw clenches, an inner war going on, but he does as I ask, even if I can see the reluctance written all over him.

If only he knew.

There is only one reason I haven't been able to say anything in return...

The second his hands are free is when I make my move. I fling myself at him, leaping up to cling around his neck, and he catches me so fucking easily.

The heat of him, the security I feel in his arms, it all washes over me, leaving my blood singing.

"Is this how you invite all your guests inside?" Luke arches an eyebrow at me.

"Just the cowboy I'm in love with." I exhale, bringing our lips together.

Luke walks us through the door, claiming me with a kiss that races straight down to my toes, leaving me a melted puddle in his arms.

I'm a koala, clung around him, and this moment is everything I'd been wishing for since I drove away from his ranch and Crimson Ridge a month ago.

"Don't move." Luke sets me down on the countertop of my tiny kitchenette, places his cowboy hat on my head—at which point I nearly straight up whimper—then disappears to shut my front door, returning with the dish he'd been carrying and another bag.

I'm an absolute slut for wearing this man's hat.

"Brad wouldn't let me come without bringing ice cream. That boy has got the world's biggest sweet tooth." He shrugs and puts the pints in the freezer while I unashamedly stare at his ass in those jeans.

As he stands there, a gruff noise comes out of him. Crouching down, he opens the fridge door, looking at the array of empty shelves.

"I should've been here sooner." Luke turns around and gives me a long look. "You're gonna let me take care of you." *Stepping closer.* "You're gonna let me love you the way you deserve." *Closer still.* "And you're gonna start learning to accept help, sweetheart."

My cowboy comes over to stand between my knees, then tilts my chin up with a crooked finger.

I want all of that... but I can't help feeling like I don't deserve it.

"You're serious, that Brad's ok with all this?" Searching his eyes, I chew the inside of my cheek. I'm so lost to this man. So in love with him, but at the same time, feel like such a shitty friend for not being the one to tell him, and it's even worse knowing that Luke has been talking to him about this for weeks.

Luke doesn't answer my question, instead he sighs and digs out his phone. "By the way, that video... I don't even want to admit how many times I've watched it over and over." Hitting me with a look of pure sin, he taps something on the screen, and my body heats, thinking back to the hottest night of my life.

Except, I don't have time to get lost in that memory because Luke holds the phone in front of his face, a video call dialing, as he watches me through dark eyes.

"Put her on, Dad. She's being weird about it, isn't she?"

Oh god. Brad's voice immediately connects at the other end of the line, and I want to dissolve into this kitchen counter.

When he turns the phone around, with a quirk tugging at the corner of his lips, the screen is filled with both Brad and Flinn's faces, who are both grinning like fools.

I peek back at them from behind my hands.

"Already *wearing the hat*, I see." He clicks his tongue, and I turn beetroot red. "If I'd known you were aiming to be my stepmother, I might have put in a good word for you with the old man years ago." Brad cackles, his face lit up with mirth.

Groans come from both me and Luke.

"Do you loathe me? You absolutely do, don't you?" I'm bracing myself for the worst.

"Skylar Addams, believe it or not, I want my best friend to be happy... besides, you don't know the *real* story of how Flinn and I got together." The two faces on screen exchange a knowing and entirely besotted with each other glance before Brad turns his attention back to me. "Anyway, I can't blame you for choosing a Rhodes man; we are superior after all. Even if you got stuck with the second best option."

"Hey." Luke protests, his voice a deep rumble I've missed so damn much.

My best friend looks far too pleased with himself, like he masterminded this entire situation.

"Ok, so enjoy your date, don't rush back tomorrow, and please for the love of all things holy do *not* tell me any details."

Brad scrunches his face up, and after blowing air kisses and suggestive winks my way, they hang up.

"Tomorrow? What's tomorrow? I blink at Luke.

"The guys are gonna take care of the ranch, said I wasn't allowed to come home unless you came with me." He sets the phone down and cups my face in two hands, brushing the apple of my cheeks with his thumbs. Giving me a tiny smile when he touches the smear of clay facemask.

"What if I didn't come with you?" I bite my lip, teasing him.

"I'm pretty sure the plan was more or less for me to keep showing up on your doorstep with food every night."

"Trying to lure me like a stray cat?"

Luke brushes over my bottom lip with a thumb, pressing down slightly and sending sparks through my blood with that move he does oh, so well.

"Trying to take care of you... to show you how much I want to take care of you."

I swallow back the thick wall of emotion threatening to rise.

"Just so you know, *tomorrow* is only because they want to see you. Brad's got this whole plan to cook you dinner and hang out. This isn't about dragging you back to Crimson Ridge, I know your life is here, and your business. I don't have the answers to all that just yet, but I think we're both smart enough to take it one step at a time and make it work."

God. I love this man beyond all reason.

"I've got one question for you..." My fingers tentatively roam up the front of his shirt.

"Anything you want, sweetheart." His words are a deep, velvety timbre.

"Would you like to see my bedroom, Mr. Rhodes?"

A wicked glint in his eyes is the only warning I get as he scoops beneath my ass and hauls me against his chest.

"If it involves you falling apart while screaming my name,

then I want to thoroughly explore every inch of this place. Repeatedly."

His lips seek my own as he walks us the short distance to my bedroom, and I direct him where to go between tugging on his hair and his clothes.

Tumbling us down onto the bed, the weight of him—pinning me down and covering my body—ignites my bloodstream. I'm panting for more, ready to beg if I need to.

"Luke…" I thread my fingers into his hair, whimpering his name. "*Please*. I missed you so much. I'm so fucking in love with you. Don't make me wait."

His dark eyes glitter at me in the soft glow of light spilling from the hallway.

"You've been my dream for so long, this time I'm not waking up… I love you, sweetheart." He drops his mouth to cover mine, letting me drag him down to line our bodies up perfectly, then murmurs softly against my mouth.

"Turns out, wishes really do come true."

EPILOGUE

Skylar

We pull into the long driveway, passing beneath the familiar wooden arch and hanging metal sign to *Rhodes Ranch*.

Luke has kept my fingers laced with his, tucked on his jean-clad thigh for the entire drive back over to Crimson Ridge as if he's worried I'm going to disappear in a puff of smoke from the front seat.

Little does this cowboy know he's got nothing to fear on that front, however, I might burst into a fiery inferno of embarrassment the second I see Brad and Flinn when we walk through that door hand in hand.

I'm still struggling to come to terms with how unexpected the past day has been, but getting to spend time with my cowboy—no matter how odd it feels to see the man without a horse or ten following him around—has been a gift I certainly am going to cling tight to.

There was also the slightly uncomfortable, but nonetheless important, step of breaking the news to my parents when they threatened to send out a search party after I avoided their first five attempts to video chat with me. My mom looked delighted, meanwhile, my father looked like he needed to go take a long walk to digest the news.

Mom gave me a wink and quietly whispered that she'd have a chat with him over crab claws and a few margaritas at their current favorite beachfront spot for dinner these days.

She also insisted that Luke fly down with me to come and vacation with them during the summer. Considering I'd barely got the words out of my mouth to say that we were together, I wasn't sure if all I'd be left with was the sight of his tail lights disappearing over the horizon.

Yet he smiled and hit her with the kind of *yes, ma'am* cowboy charm that had my own damn mother giggling and planning our itinerary before we'd hung up the phone.

I always knew she had a soft spot for the Rhodes men.

Sneaking a glance at his side profile, I can't help but wonder what he's thinking. Luke has been quiet, not awkward or anything like that, but more like he's just *content* as he rubs his thumb absently against my palm, and that makes my heart turn into a sparkling flywheel inside my chest.

However, rather than pulling up to the house straight away like I'm expecting, he stops with the motor running on a sweeping bend overlooking a part of the ranch that during spring and summer months is used as grazing pasture. I remember all the times younger me used to drive past this very point, seeing the graceful, long necks and sleek coats of the horses glinting in the sunshine as they roamed around.

"Why are we stopping?" I chew my lip.

"Grab your coat." He hops out his door, slips his hat on, and walks around to the hood of the truck.

I do as he asks, but am a little bemused.

Luke rests the ass of his perfectly fitted jeans up against the front grill, and gestures for me to come stand in front of him. I mean, I'm not gonna ever say no to being tucked in this man's embrace, so I nestle against his front, as he wraps his strong arms around me from behind.

"Is this the part where you give me the pep talk about meeting your son?" I tease.

His gruff, rich chuckle tickles my neck as he runs his lips over the sensitive patch of skin below my ear.

"You don't need to be nervous." Before I can protest, he adds, "You always make jokes when you're nervous." Intertwining our fingers together, he raises both our right hands, while keeping the other pressed firmly against my stomach. "See that slope over there, sweetheart."

I follow the direction he's pointing in and nod.

"That's south-facing." He says.

My pulse does a little skitter.

"Bet the horses love catching the sun over there." I swallow thickly.

"They do, but it's not the best pasture for them." Luke's deep voice rumbles through me. "What it *would* be perfect for is growing something that needs plenty of sunshine hours... something that doesn't mind the ice and the snow."

Hot tears prick the back of my eyes.

"Luke..." I exhale.

"You could plant as many varieties as you like there." He murmurs against my neck and I can feel the emotion bubbling up, ready to overflow with how much I love the man at my back.

"But it's such a long commitment, they take at least a full season to flower. Maybe even longer depending on when they're planted and the age of the plant itself." I don't know why I'm babbling on and making excuses. Because I don't intend on going anywhere, but what this cowboy is already offering is to help make one of my dreams come true and I don't exactly know what to do with how immense that feels.

"I'm kinda hoping you might stick around long enough to see them bloom, sweetheart."

He spins me around and cups my cheeks in both palms.

All I can do is nod and sniffle and melt under his steady gaze.

"I love you, Skylar. Grow as many peonies as you want here, let me invest in your dreams."

"You'd seriously do that? Why? I can't let you do that."

He gives me the sexiest smile and brushes his thumbs over my cheeks to swipe away the wetness gathering there.

"Because, you're gonna let me look after you, but more than that, you're gonna make those dreams all tucked away in the spreadsheets you've got in that damn phone of yours come to life." He angles his head so he can kiss me, soft, slow, standing here overlooking his ranch and I feel like I'm floating.

Pulling back, he pushes some strands of hair off my forehead, while I'm busy dissolving into a puddle.

"I want to watch you grow your dreams, Skylar because you're bringing mine to life just by being here with me."

My heart is so full it's about to burst, I swear to god.

"God, I'm so in love with you... I didn't think this moment could get any better."

His eyes dance as I say those words.

"Sweetheart, it's only just getting started."

THANK YOU FOR READING

I had so much fun with Luke and Sky and getting to write something sexy, swoony, and fluffy for them. I just wasn't ready to let them go. Want to stick around and see a little more? Grab the extended epilogue from Daddy Rhodes' POV:

https://www.elliottroseauthor.com/bonuses

Loving the Crimson Ridge world and don't want to leave? Me either... Make sure to come and join my reader group - this is where all the announcements and first peeks will be happening on any future bonus content:

https://www.facebook.com/groups/thecauldronelliottrose

—

INSTAGRAM | TIKTOK | FACEBOOK

ACKNOWLEDGEMENTS

The world of *Crimson Ridge* arrived in a creative whirlwind at the start of this year. As seems to be the pattern with all my best ideas and inspiration moments, this series galloped in during the middle of the night (when I was very much supposed to be on deadline for another book, I might add).

Almost a year later, look how far we've come. I'm so excited to share more swoony cowboys and forbidden love stories with you all.

To every single reader who has helped share the love for these characters, or press one of my books into someone's hands, I am besotted with you. Picture me swooning with heart eyes every time your share boundless creativity and excitement for an Elliott Rose character or story.

From the bottom of my heart, and from Daddy Rhodes and our girl Sky... we send you all our love.

xo

Also by Elliott Rose

Crimson Ridge

Taboo Cowboy Romance

Chasing The Wild

Braving The Storm

Taming The Heart - April 2025

Saving The Rain - 2025

Bouquets & Buckles

Port Macabre Standalones

Why Choose + Dark Romance

Where the Villains get the girl, and each other.

Vengeful Gods

Fox, Thorne, Ky, Ven - HEA Novella

Noire Moon - Prologue Novella

Macabre Gods - March 2025

Nocturnal Hearts

Dark Paranormal-Fantasy Romance, Interconnected Standalones

Sweet Inferno

(Rivals to Lovers x Novella)

In Darkness Waits Desire

(Grumpy x Sunshine)

The Queen's Temptation

(Forbidden x Shadow Daddy Bodyguard)

Vicious Cravings

(MMF x Enemies to Lovers)

Brutal Birthright

(Academy Setting, Teacher x Student)

LEAVE A REVIEW

If you enjoyed this novella, please consider taking a quick moment to leave a review. Even a couple of words are incredibly helpful and provide the sparkly fuel us Indie Romance Authors thrive on.

(Well, that and coffee)

About the Author

Elliott Rose is an indie author of romance on the deliciously dark side. She lives in a teeny tiny beachside community in the south of Aotearoa, New Zealand with her partner and three rescue dogs. Find her with a witchy brew in hand, a notebook overflowing with book ideas, or wandering along the beach.

- Join her reader group *The Cauldron* for exclusive giveaways, BTS details, first looks at character art/inspo, and intimate chats about new and ongoing projects.
- Join her Newsletter for all the goodies and major news direct to your email inbox.